A SCANDALOUS SITUATION

"Where does he live, this Mr. Traling? How often does he come here?" Lord Kinsford demanded. "I can't think what you're about, entertaining a man in your home without a chaperone."

"Oh, yes you can," Clarissa said. "You can well imagine the unseemly things that occur when Mr. Traling comes to see me at ten o'clock in the morning."

"The hour has very little to do with it," Kinsford insisted. "That sort of thing can go on at any time of day."

"I'm not aware of any stigma attached to visiting me. In fact, you seem to be the only person who has ever thought to question my virtue." Clarissa produced a plaintive sigh. "I suppose right now the villagers are saying, 'Well, what is he doing at her house at this hour of the night? *That sort of thing* could be going on at this very moment.' But you would not wish me to send you away for fear of such talk, would you?"

But even as she spoke so lightly, Clarissa felt a tremor of apprehension. She knew perfectly well that the arrogant earl had no intention of leaving—and was quite capable of trying to test her virtue to prove his point. . . .

The Village Spinster

by
Laura Matthews

A SIGNET BOOK

SIGNET
Published by the Penguin Group
Penguin Books USA Inc., 375 Hudson Street,
New York, New York 10014, U.S.A.
Penguin Books Ltd, 27 Wrights Lane,
London W8 5TZ, England
Penguin Books Australia Ltd, Ringwood,
Victoria, Australia
Penguin Books Canada Ltd, 10 Alcorn Avenue,
Toronto, Ontario, Canada M4V 3B2
Penguin Books (N.Z.) Ltd. 182-190 Wairau Road,
Auckland 10, New Zealand

Penguin Books Ltd, Registered Offices:
Harmondsworth, Middlesex, England

First published by Signet, an imprint of New American Library,
a division of Penguin Books USA Inc.

First Printing, February, 1993
10 9 8 7 6 5 4 3 2 1

For Paul, with love
and
For Kay, with thanks

1

Clarissa Driscoll was not expecting a visit from the Earl of Kinsford. It was, perhaps, the furthest thing from her mind that fine spring day. As she sipped the cup of tea Meg had brought, she was allowing her thoughts to drift to other Aprils, when she had been younger, when the view from the sitting-room window had not been a village street but the lush green of rolling lawns, with hedgerows in the distance and the home wood off to the right. There had been a much wider expanse of window to let in the sparkling sunlight then, not the cramped little box that Clarissa made do with these days. The only greenery in sight now was the vines and the leaves of the geranium plants in the window box.

Meg had remained in the doorway after her announcement and now repeated, rather impatiently, "Ma'am, it's the Earl of Kinsford. He's here in the hall." Her voice dropped to a hiss as she stretched her neck inside the door while trying to keep the visitor from hearing her. "What am I to do with him?"

"Well, I suppose you must show him in," Clarissa said, frowning. She knew Alexander Barrington, Fifth Earl of Kinsford, from the old days, of course, when she had been more of a social equal, and knew, from his half-brother and half-sister, that he was temporarily at Kinsford Hall.

"Yes, ma'am." Meg made a gesture toward her that Clarissa did not understand and when she stared blankly at the girl, Meg hissed, "Your cap, ma'am!"

"What's the matter with it?"

"You don't want to wear it when the earl is here," Meg informed her sternly.

"Why ever not? It's a perfectly acceptable cap. I haven't had it more than a fortnight."

With a snort of disgust, Meg slipped back out through the door, returning almost immediately to announce, in her most impressive imitation of Clarissa's own genteel accent, "The Earl of Kinsford, Miss Driscoll."

When Clarissa graciously rose to greet her visitor, she remembered that she had kicked off her slippers to curl her feet under her as she sat and stared out the window. It was with a certain chagrin that she noticed Kinsford's gaze travel almost immediately to her stocking feet. Clarissa did not apologize for things like forgetting to wear her shoes to welcome visitors. According to her deceased father, it was a waste of time to apologize for such minor infractions of social rules.

"Lord Kinsford. It must be several years since I've seen you. At the time of your father's death, perhaps."

"Probably. I haven't been home much recently." Though Lord Kinsford had raised his eyes from her feet to her face, his expression retained an element of astonishment.

In his top boots and breeches, he looked younger than his thirty years. He had always been a handsome man, of course. A great credit to the Barrington looks, the villagers were wont to say. Clarissa's first recollection of him was as a boy of eight, a solid little fellow, given to neck-or-nothing riding and pursuits of rabbits with a gun he was much too young to carry. Not that he had frightened her then any more than he did now.

"Won't you sit down? Perhaps you'd like a cup of tea. I was just having mine."

"Thank you, no." He chose the only truly comfortable chair in the room. It was the one Clarissa invariably sat in, though today she'd been on the sofa. She resumed her seat there, considered tucking her feet up under her again, and decided against it. But she wasn't going to go fiddling around on the floor with her feet, either, trying to find her shoes and slip into them. He hadn't, after all, given any warning of his visit.

Lord Kinsford was observing her closely. She could tell this despite his hooded eyes and the deceptive casualness of his posture in the chair. He had draped one buckskin-clad leg over the other, both stretched out in front of him so informally that she wondered if he were attempting to duplicate her own lack of propriety. Since he said nothing, after a minute of silence she raised her brows inquiringly. She had been told once, by a nervous singing pupil, that this expression made her look positively forbidding. Clarissa doubted that. Certainly the earl was unlikely to be intimidated.

"I've come about Aria and Will, as you must realize," he said at length.

His half-brother and half-sister were very well-known to her, since Lady Aria came for singing, drawing, and watercolor lessons, as well as instruction on the pianoforte. Both Lady Aria and Master

William learned the latest dances from her, there being no dancing master in the neighborhood. The younger Barringtons bore a certain resemblance to the earl, their guardian. They had the same blue eyes and high foreheads, though lighter hair than his. And not the determined chin. Clarissa remembered the chin even from the boy of eight. He should grow a beard, she thought, to disguise that chin. One look at it and you knew without a doubt that he was stubborn and spoiled, that he always intended to have his way. And that he tolerated no nonsense.

"I'd be happy to give you a report on their progress. Lady Aria is a delightful child, but not particularly talented upon the pianoforte. I wouldn't discontinue her lessons, however. It's an accomplishment that she'll need to possess, even if she never plays more than moderately well, nor sings with any particular charm. On the other hand, she has rather a special endowment so far as watercolors are concerned. Have you seen any of her drawings?"

"I don't believe so." He was frowning slightly, the assessing eyes less hooded now, but the corners of his mouth tight. "It was not about her artwork that I came."

"No? Ah, their dancing lessons. The two of them are delightful, you know. Master William has a certain grace that few his age manage to achieve. It's true that he tends to be more energetic than absolutely necessary, but that will come under control in time. Lady Aria could execute any dance in her sleep, she's so in tune with the music and so gifted in movement. Never makes a misstep. There aren't very many young people who can see a dance once and remember every step and gesture that way. I believe it must be a talent much as I've heard some people can read the page of a book and retain an image of the whole page in their minds.''

''It isn't about their dancing that I've come, either.''

Clarissa hadn't actually thought it was. She had not been on this earth for seven-and-twenty years without picking up a little facility at judging the moods of her contemporaries. Lord Kinsford was irritated. Once, when they were more or less equals in the neighborhood, that would not have mattered. Now, when she depended on the income from her lessons, his irritation could threaten her way of life. There was not an unlimited supply of gentlefolk needing her services, and Lady Aria and Master William were the mainstay of her precarious independence.

Lord Kinsford lifted one hand partially off the leg where it had rested. It was a very small gesture, and Clarissa knew that it was meant to indicate that he had finished listening to her and was ready to speak. As gestures go, this one was particularly offensive to her, like a command to be still and listen to The Word from on High. His father had been much the same sort of autocratic man.

His voice was a remarkably smooth baritone. He kept his eyes squarely on her face to impress her with the seriousness of his subject. ''It has come to my attention that Will and Aria, in the process of racing one another across Barnet Park, managed to stray onto John Olsen's land, where they destroyed a newly plowed field, as well as frightening the plow horses and plowboy.''

He paused, as though expecting Clarissa to say something. When she merely regarded him with moderate attention, he continued. ''Mr. Olsen was very distressed about the matter, as I believe you are aware.''

Again he paused and again she said nothing.

"Come now. I believe you happened to be walking near the park and witnessed the whole altercation.''

"Yes.''

"Mr. Olsen informed me that you sided with the children and their wild spirits, convincing him that they meant no harm.''

"Well, they didn't.''

"It was thoughtless and careless of them. Olsen is a tenant of mine and cannot afford to have his plantings destroyed.''

"The agreement we reached was that the children would reimburse Mr. Olsen for the seed and the plowboy's time from their allowances. I trust they upheld their end of the bargain.''

"Yes.'' His lips tightened. "Mr. Olsen also,'' Lord Kinsford said, his eyes sharp, "indicated that you had reminded him of my own escapades at their age and convinced him that there was no need to pass along the tale to me. The inference being that I wouldn't regard their conduct with displeasure.''

Clarissa nodded. "Yes, I believe that's why I mentioned it.''

"But I do find something wrong with their conduct, Miss Driscoll.''

"Naturally.''

"You tried to prevent me from giving them a well-deserved dressing-down.''

"Yes.'' Clarissa continued to regard him with mild interest, mostly because she knew it would irritate him further.

"I consider that undermining my authority.''

"But, Lord Kinsford, you weren't here when the event took place a month ago. It was the sort of occasion that needed to be handled promptly to assure fairness all around. Mr. Olsen could have written to you in London and explained the matter, but it hardly seemed necessary."

Kinsford gripped his knees as he leaned forward to stress his words. "They're my brother and sister. I'm responsible for their conduct, whether I'm at Kinsford Hall or not. Even their mother would not have condoned such ramshackle behavior. And yet you managed to keep the whole matter silent, to let them think they could behave in such a fashion if they chose."

"Come, come, Lord Kinsford. I did no such thing. You should be here to thank me, not to scold me for my handling of the matter." Clarissa tapped a finger on the arm of the sofa, a sure sign to those who knew her well—which was not the case with Lord Kinsford—that her patience was near an end. "I not only made them repay Mr. Olsen for his losses, I convinced Master William to give the plowboy a shilling for the trouble caused him. A rather healthy chunk, in all, of his weekly allotment. And, much as it pained me, I also lectured Lady Aria on the view the quality would take of her hoydenish behavior. All in all, a very good day's work, if I do say so myself."

Kinsford rose from the overstuffed chair and walked restlessly around the small room. "It's not that I don't appreciate your attempt to assist the children, Miss Driscoll. It's the effort at secrecy that distresses me. Their mother should have been advised of the incident. She is not without influence with her children. And she would, certainly, have notified me so that I could handle things myself.''

''You would have done something different?'' Clarissa asked sweetly.

He stood with his back to her, staring out into the street. The rumble of a passing cart made it impossible for him to speak immediately. When the noise had died away, he turned to her, grimaced, and said, ''I won't quibble with the arrangements you made. They were adequate. Why didn't you tell Lady Kinsford?''

''Me?'' Clarissa regarded him with astonishment. ''You expected me to tattle on your brother and sister? How absurd! Your stepmama would have considered it impertinent in me to do any such thing. And I am not at all sure she would have grasped the problem. Perhaps Master William and Lady Aria should have told her themselves. I'm sure I can't answer for that.''

She could see the frustration in his eyes. He remained in front of the window, framed against the sunlight, considering her. His brows were drawn down and his mouth slightly pursed. Clarissa realized that he was probably deciding whether she had so overstepped her position that she should be dismissed as the youngsters' teacher. This was the time to conciliate him, but he had set her back up and she found she couldn't even manage an amiable smile. She returned his gaze coolly.

''You make it difficult for me, Miss Driscoll. I sense that were the same thing to happen again, you would handle it precisely the same way.''

''Certainly. Though I must say that it's unlikely I shall be in a position to do so on another occasion.''

''True.'' The force of this argument apparently

weighed with him. He shrugged his solid shoulders and moved a step toward her. "Very well. For the time being, they will continue their lessons. They both seem to enjoy them."

Relieved, Clarissa rose, only to remember once again that she wasn't wearing her slippers. This time she managed to work her feet into them as she talked. "Perhaps you would care to see some of Lady Aria's watercolors before you leave. She has quite a keen eye and a delightful sense of fun. No baskets of fruit or landscape scenes for her. The subject matter she chooses is charmingly unusual. This one, for instance."

Clarissa moved easily across the room to an artist's stand on which several sheets of paper rested. She picked up the one titled "Returning from a Dinner Party at Night" in which there were several people on horseback, some in an open carriage, and even two walking. The colors were vivid and pleasing to the eye. The scene flowed cheerfully past as though one were watching a parade of one's neighbors.

With casual grace, Lord Kinsford stepped across to take the watercolor from her hands. He regarded it for several minutes without speaking, then set it down and picked up another from the stand. Pausing the longest over one of a riding party, he eventually returned them all to their place. "Delightful," he pronounced in a voice at once surprised and pleased. "I had no idea Aria had the patience to sit as long as it would take to produce such artwork."

"She's quite absorbed when she's working. I've known her to pass up a whole plate of cream cakes."

"Goodness." The earl smiled slightly. "Not a

common occurrence, in my experience. I take it this enthusiasm does not extend to the pianoforte.''

''No.''

''Ah, well, one can only expect so much of a fifteen-year-old girl.'' He bowed slightly to her. ''I'll take my leave, then, Miss Driscoll.''

Clarissa walked behind him to the sitting-room door and watched as he picked up his riding gauntlets from the hall table. As she had expected, Meg hovered near the front door, ready with Lord Kinsford's curly-brimmed beaver hat and his riding crop. The girl was a bit in awe of his lordship, but curious. Her eyes took in every detail of his dress and expression, presumably for relating it subsequently to her family on the farm.

When the door was closed cautiously behind him, Meg happened to glance over and see Clarissa still wriggling her foot to get it comfortably into the soft gray slipper. ''Oh, ma'am, you weren't without your shoes, surely!'' she exclaimed. ''What will his lordship think of us?''

''Nothing flattering, I assure you,'' she said dryly. ''But we don't care, do we?''

Meg refused to reply to this teasing rejoinder. She was truly shocked by her employer's lack of concern. For Meg had ambitions. Perhaps she hoped, in time, to find a place at Kinsford Hall along with her sister; or eventually, to be a lady's maid to some London matron. Putting on such an exhibition as today's before the earl himself, she could not but believe, was a sadly ramshackle way of going on, and she felt a certain responsibility for her mistress.

Clarissa had finally wedged her second foot back into its slipper. With a gesture of dismissal she disposed of the earl's visit, saying to Meg, ''Never

mind. He's a little high in the instep these days."
Then she mused more to herself than the maid,
"Though I can't imagine what possesses him to be.
Any high spirits in Lady Aria and Master William
pale by comparison with his own at that age." When
Meg continued to regard her with a dubious expres-
sion, Clarissa sighed. "You may take away the tea
things, Meg."

2

Outside the cottage, Lord Kinsford swung onto his horse, which had been held for him by a village urchin whose name he could not recall. Delighted with the coin Kinsford tossed him, the boy tugged respectfully at his forelock. Quite a contrast to Miss Driscoll's cool attitude toward a man who employed her, Lord Kinsford thought, his brow creasing in an unconscious frown.

He'd forgotten what Clarissa Driscoll was like, though he'd known her as a child. Thinking back, he remembered her as a spirited girl, with a captivating oval face and sparkling gray eyes. For many years his visits to Kinsford Hall had been infrequent and of short duration, and he'd seldom seen or spoken to her.

Five years previously her father had died, and his gambling debts had forced the sale of his estate, Pennhurst, leaving his only child with scarcely enough to purchase a small cottage in the village. Miss Driscoll had withdrawn from county society. The Pennwick village gossip was that she had doted on her father, reckless wastrel that he had been. And when she'd taken up giving lessons to augment her tiny income, the villagers came to regard her as a kind of genteel eccentric.

Lord Kinsford snorted. She would certainly be viewed as an oddity if she made a practice of greeting visitors without shoes! And that ludicrous cap! She couldn't be above seven-and-twenty, only a few years short of his own thirty. The cap would be her concession to neighborhood custom, he supposed, but it looked bizarre perched precariously on her wreath of glossy brown hair. More likely it was an affectation, meant to suggest that she considered herself a determined spinster, her attractions past their prime.

If that was so, she was far out, he decided. She was still more than handsome enough, with her braids wrapped tidily about her head, her gray eyes large and well-set above a patrician nose and full lips. Her figure was excellent. But spinster she undoubtedly was, at her age. He couldn't recall hearing of her ever being seriously courted, even before her father's death. It would be a pity if she were to dwindle into the village oddity.

A rueful smile twitched his lips. He'd intended, out of respect for their former association, to have a simple chat with Clarissa, in the friendliest manner, and clarify just what was expected of her in her relations with Aria and Will. She should have been in a state of nerves, anticipating that at any time he would descend upon her and chastise her for her conduct over the Farmer Olsen incident. He'd come unannounced just so she wouldn't be thrown unnecessarily into palpitations. Instead, somehow she'd managed to turn things around so he'd had little to say. Now that he came to think about it, she'd had the effrontery to damn near toy with him!

He grinned and flicked the reins to urge his horse, Longbridge, on. Kinsford couldn't help but wonder if he'd sent a note ahead whether she would have put on her shoes.

As he rode through the village of Pennwick, Kinsford was aware of the twitching of curtains at cottage windows. He knew the villagers were curious about him. There were always rumors when he came home: he was about to be married, he had decided to take his half-brother and half-sister to town with him, he was selling off the south pasture because he needed the money. Heaven knew where the rumors arose; probably over a pint of beer. It was never necessary to deny them. By his actions, they could see that he was not marrying, or taking his siblings to town, or selling off property. Besides, he usually managed, when he was at home, to visit the old county families and they in turn depressed any untoward rumors.

There was nothing Kinsford's stepmother liked better than asking him to execute a commission for her ''when he was in the village.'' On this occasion she had requested that he match some thread for her, a totally inappropriate task for one of his position, of course, but he seldom refused her, knowing that what she liked second-best was to complain in a mild but heartbreaking manner of her disappointment with his treatment of her and her children. He had never let such behavior disturb him, but something Miss Driscoll had said had alerted him that there might be something amiss here. Would Lady Kinsford really not have been concerned about the children's misbehavior?

Kinsford dismounted in front of the shop and tied Longbridge to the iron ring provided. Actually, he had brought Aria with him, leaving her in the village when he went to visit Miss Driscoll. Entering the shop now, he found her deep in conversation with Mrs. Luden.

"I should think it's close enough," Lady Aria commented, wrapping two bits of thread around her finger side by side. "Still, we'd best take the other spool as well, just in case. One or the other must have been what she bought before."

Kinsford was always surprised to find his half-sister so practical. And so pretty. Unlike himself, she was blond and small and soft-edged. To look at her one would not have suspected the mischief she could manage. And she was obviously mature for her age, no longer the child he remembered from other visits. Kinsford strongly suspected that, in another year, he was going to have to take her up to London for a Season. And taking her meant taking the dowager as well. A daunting thought.

"Very wise," he said now, dipping his hand into his pocket for more coins. "Your mama will certainly approve of one of them."

This made his half-sister grin at him. "No, but it will keep her from sending a note round to pester Mrs. Luden."

"Lady Kinsford never pesters me," Mrs. Luden said stoutly. "She's a particular lady, to be sure, but most gracious."

Lady Aria remembered where her brother had just been and teased, "No doubt you found Miss Driscoll most gracious, also."

"Without her shoes," he muttered, just barely audible.

Lady Aria bit her lip and said nothing, but her eyes sparkled with delight. Mrs. Luden handed her a small parcel with both spools of thread and wished them a good day. Lord Kinsford took his sister's elbow, guiding her past piles of yard goods and food. Only when they had mounted their horses did Lady Aria ask, "What did you mean, without her shoes?"

"Miss Driscoll wasn't expecting me. I dare say she had forgotten she'd removed them," he admitted. "But, still, Aria. She's turned into a rather unconventional sort of woman, I suspect. I'm not at all sure she's an appropriate person to be instructing you."

Immediately Lady Aria's face clouded over. "She's the most refreshing person in the whole village, Kinsford. Everyone else is so wretchedly deferential, you want to choke. And she isn't employed to teach us manners, for heaven's sake. Please don't say you're going to cut off my lessons with her."

"I doubt your mother would approve."

"Oh, pooh! Mama could not possibly object to Miss Driscoll. There is no one in the area who could teach me so many things—art and pianoforte and dancing. Miss Driscoll has a talent at each of them, which she is able to convey with enthusiasm." Aria cocked her head engagingly. "And she's so kind to me, Kinsford, and really interested in what I do. She *listens* to me. No one else really listens to me."

Kinsford had not realized that Aria was lonely now that she had left school. He sighed. "I dare say you're old enough not to be unduly influenced by an oddity or two," he admitted, "but I don't at all like Miss Driscoll interfering in your lives outside her sphere. If that should happen again . . ."

He let the sentence hang unfinished in the crisp spring air, a threat of a sort. Not that he intended to be around to carry it out. How could he, in London, hear of the doings of one odd woman in Pennwick? Still, he hoped to impress Aria with his seriousness.

She mustn't be allowed to run wild. He would have a word with the dowager.

Lady Aria looked up at him from under the brim of her royal-blue riding bonnet. "Did Miss Driscoll show you any of my watercolors?" she asked diffidently.

"Yes, indeed," he said, relieved to change the subject. "They're quite extraordinary, Aria. I had no idea you were so talented. Perhaps we should find you a real drawing master."

Again her face clouded, and her jaw set stubbornly. "Miss Driscoll is a wonderful teacher. Any drawing master you got me would only let me paint pretty pictures of flowers or the view over the garden. I should hate that! If I can't have Miss Driscoll, I won't have anyone!"

Kinsford's back stiffened. "You forget yourself, Aria. Any such decision remains with me."

She did not reply. With a mutinous glare, she urged her horse to the gallop. Firebird was one of the finest mares the estate had produced in many years, and she quickly outdistanced his own Longbridge, since Kinsford refused to give chase to the girl. It was most certainly unnecessary, and beneath his dignity. Aria's outright rudeness was a disagreeable surprise. Something really would have to be done about her lack of manners.

His half-sister was a neck-or-nothing rider. He watched as she put Firebird to the hedge at the side of the road. Firebird sailed over another hedge and a stream a few paces beyond with the greatest ease. Lady Aria sat her horse as well as any woman Kinsford had ever seen and he felt a flash of pride in her.

Out of the corner of his eye Lord Kinsford saw a motion in the long grasses to his left, not far from the stream Firebird was approaching. It was doubt-less a fox or a dog—nothing to be alarmed about. Except that Firebird's one fault was her skittishness.

Horse and rider were aimed directly at the hidden animal. Lady Aria raised her hands to urge Firebird over a low fence. As Firebird rose from the ground, the dog rushed at her, barking ferociously. Horse and rider seemed poised for an instant over the fence. But Firebird had lost her stride in her nervous attempt to shy away from the animal. A hoof caught the top rung of the fence and she landed awkwardly, stumbling to the left.

Lady Aria, caught off-guard, had the reins yanked out of her grip. Kinsford watched helplessly as she was hurtled from the saddle and flew through the air. Before she even landed, he had dug his heels into Longbridge's sides. He saw Lady Aria hit the ground. She remained motionless. Icy fear gripped him.

Firebird stood shuddering over the girl. The dog barked on the opposite side of the fence. Longbridge soared over the hedges, over the stream, and finally over the fence. Kinsford was out of the saddle before he had even stopped his horse.

"Aria! My God, Aria, are you all right?"

But the girl was silent.

Kinsford knelt down beside her and took her wrist in his hand. He could feel a faint pulse. Her face seemed unbearably white where she lay twisted onto her side, one shoulder at an awkward angle. With careful fingers he felt along her head first, where he could see a swelling at her temple. There was no broken skin but the swelling seemed alarmingly large. Undoubtedly, the blow to her head had rendered her unconscious. Kinsford quickly ran his hands over the dislocated shoulder and along her arms and legs, but only the left wrist was puffed up. Her boots prevented any assessment of her ankles, but they would probably have provided protection.

He had helped men with dislocated shoulders on the battlefield, but his sister looked so very small and fragile, he was tempted to wait until a doctor could attempt the reduction. But that meant a considerable wait, and Aria might regain consciousness in the meantime. Far better to manage it now before the excruciating pain descended upon her.

Bracing himself, and making sure that her shoulder was firmly lodged against the ground, Kinsford quickly manipulated the shoulder back into position. The sound of the pop, and the agonized groan that was forced from Aria left him somewhat shaken. Kinsford sat back on his haunches, trying to decide what to do next.

It was more than a mile to the Hall. He could leave Aria and go for a doctor, or go for a cart to bring her home. But the idea of leaving her alone in the field was horrifying to him. She might awaken in terrible pain and not understand what was happening. She might even try to rise and make her way home. The village was closer than Kinsford Hall. He could more easily carry her there and send for a doctor, as well as a cart to take her home. But was it wise to carry her with a possibly broken wrist?

There really didn't seem to be much choice. Kinsford stripped off his coat and his cravat, wound the former around the shoulder to hold it in place and bound the wrist with the latter. His sister moaned softly as he lifted her from the ground into his arms, tucking her shoulder tightly against his body. The horses could make their way home or follow him into the village; it was a matter of total indifference to him.

He was a man of average height and solid, athletic physique. Carrying the girl was not a particular strain for him, but trying not to jostle her complicated matters somewhat. When he lost his hat in picking her up, he left it where it fell. His boots were soon muddy from the damp fields, even though he managed to find a footbridge across the stream. His breeches were splattered and his shirt crumpled by the time he reached the outskirts of Pennwick village.

It had been Lord Kinsford's intention to take the girl to Mrs. Luden, who lived behind her shop, but the first cottage he passed was that of Miss Driscoll and something made him hesitate there, before her door. The argument he'd had with his sister had involved Miss Driscoll and it seemed to Kinsford that his sister would have chosen her over Mrs. Luden to offer succor at such a time. Doubtful as he was himself, he determined for his sister's sake to seek help there. With his elbow he managed to bang gracelessly on the door.

Meg's eyes widened when she saw his lordship with Lady Aria in his arms. "Oh, my lord!" she exclaimed. "What's happened? Bring her in straightaway. Miss Driscoll! Miss Driscoll!"

The urgency of the summons brought Clarissa almost instantly into the tiny hallway. She took in the scene at a glance and pointed to the sitting-room door. "Bring her in here. Meg, send Jimmy for Dr. Lawrence right away, please."

"What happened?" Clarissa asked as she carefully loosened the neck of Lady Aria's riding costume. The girl was still unconscious, her face pale, and her breathing shallow.

"She fell from her horse. A dog frightened Firebird as they were just beginning a jump." He touched the swollen area on the side of Lady Aria's head. "There were no rocks in the area. Still, she must have hit the ground hard enough to do this."

"And her shoulder?"

"It was dislocated, but I've restored it. Unless the walk here has thrown it out again."

"Let's have a look at it." Clarissa unwound the coat and ran her fingers along the shoulder. She made a moue of distress. "There's a lot of bruising, but it seems to be in place now. She's fortunate you knew how to do it. It will save her a great deal of pain."

He nodded. "Her wrist is swollen, too. I can't tell if it's broken."

Clarissa removed the cravat and felt along the wrist. "I'd guess not, but it's hard to tell. I'll prepare a poultice in hot moist flannels for her head and we should keep her warm because of the shock. You'll find a blanket in the closet at the head of the stairs." She seemed to recollect herself. "Or you may wait a moment and Meg will get it. If Jimmy isn't off somewhere, she won't be long."

Lord Kinsford didn't hesitate. "I'll get the blanket."

She nodded and tucked a stray curl of brown hair up under her cap as she pushed through the door to the back hall. Kinsford frowned down at his sister briefly, then moved to the front hall. Just as he began to climb the stairs, there was a knock at the door. Realizing that Meg was out of the house and Miss Driscoll in the kitchen, he returned to open the door.

"The new butler, I presume," said the young man who stood there, his eyes twinkling. "My own butler generally wears a coat and neckcloth, which I believe my wife insists upon. Miss Driscoll, however, is singular enough to have a butler who answers the door in his shirtsleeves,'' the fellow mused. ''Is she home, by any chance?''

Lord Kinsford gave the man a stony look. ''Miss Driscoll is occupied at the moment. Please call another time.'' He began to close the door.

''Here now! Tell her Mr. Traling is here. I'm sure she'll see me. We're quite good friends.''

''You are, are you? Then you may wait in the hall until she's free to speak with you.'' Beneath his breath he muttered ''impertinent young pup'' as he took the stairs two at a time. There were several blankets in the closet and Kinsford decided to bring all of them. He threw a black look at the fellow still standing in the hall when he returned downstairs.

''Is there some difficulty? Perhaps I could help,'' the man suggested, though diffidently.

His lordship dismissed him curtly. ''I very much doubt it.''

He carried the blankets into the sitting room, not realizing that the young man had followed him until the fellow said, ''My word! She's not dead, is she?''

Kinsford gave him a fulminating look but just then Miss Driscoll appeared in the doorway with a steaming flannel. ''Mr. Traling,'' she said when her gaze fell on the newcomer. ''I had no idea you were here. We're a bit disorganized at present. I'm afraid I shan't be able to talk with you.''

As Kinsford tucked the blankets around his sister's still form, he was annoyed to see that Traling showed no sign of taking the hint.

''Two blankets will make her too hot,'' Traling said. ''It's a warm day.''

The earl glared at him, but Miss Driscoll merely shook her head. "Not to worry. The doctor will be here soon, and Lord Kinsford has already seen to the dislocated shoulder."

"Is this the artist?" Mr. Traling asked Miss Driscoll. "I recognize her from your drawing."

"Yes." Clarissa placed the warm poultice over the swollen and bruised area of the girl's head. "And this is her older brother, the Earl of Kinsford. Lord Kinsford, Mr. Steven Traling."

"Very pleased to meet you, my lord." Mr. Traling held out his hand, which it seemed for a moment the earl would refuse. After a barely acceptable pause, Kinsford shook hands peremptorily, his eyes narrowed first at Traling and then at Miss Driscoll, who ignored his inspection.

Lady Aria was coming around now, making little mewling sounds like a kitten. The two men turned to look at the girl, Traling with curiosity and Kinsford with concern. Clarissa soothed the girl's forehead. "You're here with me, dear," she said softly. "At Miss Driscoll's house. Your brother has brought you after a riding accident."

Lady Aria blinked her eyes open but allowed them to drift shut again with a moan. Kinsford's hands clenched at his sides. "I really think Mr. Traling will be in the way when the doctor comes," he said.

"I think I've missed the worst of it, if you've already fixed her dislocated shoulder," Mr. Traling mused. "Once, when I was a small lad, I dislocated my shoulder and it was incredibly painful when the doctor and my father rammed it back into place. I thought they were trying to snap me in two."

"Miss Driscoll, I really must insist!" Kinsford exclaimed, just as there was a loud pounding at the door. "What the devil is going on here?"

"I'll take care of that," Mr. Traling offered, obviously unoffended by Kinsford's insistence. "At least I'm not in my shirtsleeves."

3

To Clarissa's disappointment, it was not Meg with the doctor, but the Honorable William Barrington, Lady Aria's other brother. "What are the horses doing loose?" she head him demand in the hall. "Where's Lady Aria? She would never let Firebird run wild. Who are you? Where's Miss Driscoll?"

Though Mr. Traling did attempt to answer these questions, he didn't have many answers and William became impatient with him. The newest visitor strode into the sitting room, demanding Miss Driscoll's attention. When he saw his sister lying pale on the sofa, he must have known a moment's terror.

"You've killed her!" he yelled, apparently at Kinsford. "How could you do that? You've only been home two days!"

While Clarissa realized that he spoke out of shock, his older brother looked stunned at such an accusation. "She fell from her horse," he said stiffly.

"But she's an excellent rider!" Master William exclaimed.

Clarissa tried to point out the most pertinent fact. "She's not dead, Master William. She's been unconscious most of the time, which is fortunate, since her shoulder was dislocated. Meg is sending Jimmy for Dr. Lawrence."

At which statement Meg herself appeared in the doorway to announce, "The doctor's gone to Stanton Prior and they don't know when he'll be back."

Both Mr. Traling and William offered to find him. William was an even more daring rider than his sister, but he was naturally the earl's choice. "William, you go. I'll stay here with Aria."

"I'll take Firebird, then, shall I?" William asked, distractedly drawing a hand through his blond curls. "I've been galloping Rannoch pretty hard this morning."

"Take Longbridge. Firebird may still be too nervous from the accident."

"Take Longbridge?" William repeated, astonished. "You've never let anyone ride Longbridge."

Kinsford gritted his teeth. "Just take him. Get a move on or I'll go myself."

"Yes, sir," William replied, almost snapping to attention, as if his brother were still in the army with Wellington. "I'll be back in no time."

He had flung out of the room before Kinsford could say, "And don't do anything reckless." The front door slammed so hard it rattled the whole house.

"I'll heat another flannel," Meg said, and left.

Clarissa continued to sooth the partially conscious Lady Aria's forehead. Kinsford paced restlessly. Mr. Traling stood far back but the earl encountered him in his pacing and threw Clarissa a scowling look. "I wonder, Mr. Traling, if you would do a favor for me," Clarissa asked after a moment. "I feel certain the doctor will prescribe a black draught immediately and I haven't any. Would you see if Mrs. Luden has any from the apothecary?"

"What's a black draught?" he asked, curious. "Will she know what to give me?"

"Yes. There are two ways to make it but either will be fine. I myself prefer the tincture of senna with cardamom and spirit of lavender, but the epsom salts and coriander seed work just as well, I believe."

"I'm more than happy to get it," Traling said. "If Mrs. Luden hasn't any, shall I go to the apothecary in Bath?"

"No, we'll make do," Clarissa assured him.

Mr. Traling left cheerfully, just as though he hadn't been snubbed by his lordship several times since his arrival. Clarissa turned to the earl.

"Would you help me with her riding boots? She might be more comfortable."

Kinsford stepped forward to help. The boots were tight and Lady Aria moaned when he attempted to remove them. Kinsford desisted, saying, "It's too painful for her."

"No, no. Let's get them off. It will be easier on her when she's half-conscious than when she comes fully awake."

Kinsford regarded her doubtfully for a moment and then nodded. It was, after all, precisely his reasoning when he had relocated his sister's shoulder. When the boots were eventually off, he ran his fingers along the ankle. "I don't feel anything broken, just the swelling. The boots probably protected her."

Lady Aria's eyes flickered open again. "What are you doing to my foot?" she whispered anxiously. "I hurt all over. Where am I?"

Clarissa stepped into the girl's line of vision. "You're at my house, dear. You've taken a fall from your horse."

"Firebird! Is she all right?"

"Perfectly," Kinsford replied.

"I should hate myself if anything had happened to her," she whispered. "I didn't mean to hurt . . ." But her voice failed from the effort and her eyelids drooped with fatigue. Soon she seemed to be asleep.

Clarissa took a pillow from the spindle-back chair and tucked it under Lady Aria's foot. Meg placed a warm poltice on her head. Though the two women said nothing, a glance passed between them which indicated their mutual knowledge of Lady Aria's starts. Neither of them looked to Kinsford for an explanation, and it would not have occurred to him to provide one.

They heard a discreet knock at the door and Meg ushered the doctor and William directly to the sitting room. Clarissa offered the older man her hand. "Thank you for coming, sir. I hope Master William hasn't pressed you too hard."

Dr. Lawrence was a short, stocky fellow with an incurably genial face. "He did no more than protest the urgency of the matter." His hand had already gone to take Lady Aria's wrist and her eyes fluttered open. "And how are you doing, my dear? Feeling wretched, I dare say."

"Yes," she admitted. Her voice was alarmingly weak.

"Do you know what year it is?" the doctor asked.

"Eighteen-nineteen."

"And where you are?"

"In Miss Driscoll's sitting room."

"And who you are?"

"Lady Aria Barrington."

"Good." The doctor smiled. "Already I'm encouraged. We should apply a lotion to the scalp here over the blow, however. Sal-ammoniac and vinegar in whisky, diluted. Perhaps it would be best to shave the area first.''

Silent tears pooled in Lady Aria's eyes. Dr. Lawrence relented. ''Well, it is not absolutely necessary. Now, what I would like is to clear the room so that I may examine my patient. You may stay, Miss Driscoll.''

Though Kinsford looked skeptical, he joined the others without protest. Dr. Lawrence winked at Clarissa. ''Rather a lot of company for you,'' he suggested. ''If you'll give me a hand here.''

He allowed Clarissa to serve as his assistant as he did a thorough examination of his patient. Lady Aria groaned in protest at the pokings and proddings. ''Good girl,'' he said, patting her hand and turning to Clarissa. ''I'm fairly certain the ankle isn't broken, but Lady Aria should stay off it as much as possible for a few days to let it mend.''

He considered his patient thoughtfully, stroking his chin. ''I'm not sure I can recommend your removal to Kinsford Hall as yet, my dear,'' he told her. ''The blow to your head could be significant. We want to see that you remain as still as possible for a while. Any conveyance would be very painful for your shoulder, and unwise for your head. Should you mind very much?''

''Of course not,'' Lady Aria said stoutly. ''But it would be a terrible inconvenience for Miss Driscoll. We couldn't possibly impose so on her good nature.''

Clarissa laughed. ''It's no imposition at all. You won't be as comfortable here as you would at the Hall but, on the other hand, William won't be here to egg you on to mischief.''

''And Alexander won't be able to ring a peal over

my head, either,'' Lady Aria agreed. ''It sounds perfectly delightful.''

''Hardly that,'' Dr. Lawrence assured her. ''You're going to ache like the devil for the next few days. I'll come by tomorrow to see how you go on.''

In the small music room off the sitting room he explained to Clarissa and the earl that Lady Aria's remaining at Miss Driscoll's cottage was purely a precautionary measure. ''Sometimes there's damage that shows up later. What you have to watch for is disorientation. But she seems all right now and we'll hope for the best. Laudanum for the pain if needed; a little thin gruel if she gets hungry.''

Reluctantly Kinsford agreed that his sister should stay. It rankled that he would be indebted to Miss Driscoll in such a fashion, but he would not take chances with his sister's health.

The doctor had barely departed when there was a great commotion outside the cottage. Apparently Mr. Traling had returned at precisely the same time as Lady Kinsford arrived. Clarissa heard the dowager's stentorian tones demanding, ''Who are you? Where is my daughter?''

Once again Mr. Traling explained that he was an acquaintance of Miss Driscoll's and that Lady Aria was in the sitting room. The dowager appeared instantly in the doorway, where she caught one glimpse of her daughter and cried out, ''Oh, my poor child! What have they done to you?''

Lord Kinsford, who might or might not have been the one held responsible, had no choice but to provide some explanation. ''Lady Aria has taken a fall from her horse, ma'am. The doctor has seen her and feels she will be fine, though she must remain here for a day or two.''

"Here? Absurd. She must come home at once."
The dowager was not much above five-and-thirty.
She was a good-looking woman, and she had a distinct flair for the dramatic. Like a Covent Garden
actress she wrung her hands and moaned with despair. "Oh, she has injured her head. My poor,
sweet Aria. I must pray she has done no damage to
her brain." Tears welled up in her pale blue eyes.
"Oh, I could not bear that. Such a quick, bright
young thing as she is."

Meg had drawn a chair near the sofa and the dowager adjusted her lime-green skirts as she sat down
on it. When she went to take the girl's hand, she
shrieked, "Her wrist! Oh, her wrist is enormously
swollen! There are broken bones. I know there are.
She shall never be quite right again and it is all
the fault of that wild horse of hers." She glared at
Kinsford. "You should never have given her a wild
horse."

"Firebird is not a wild horse," retorted that ma-
ligned gentleman. "And Aria is an excellent rider."

"Then how did she take a fall?" demanded Lady
Kinsford.

"A dog frightened the horse just as she was beginning to jump. It was a most unfortunate accident."

Clarissa felt it was time to change the subject.
Since it was midday, she offered the dowager something to eat and drink. Lady Kinsford considered her
with a frown. "Yes, I will take a cup of tea. China,
not black. And perhaps a spot of cheese with my
bread. A soft cheese, mind. I can't tolerate those
hard cheeses, nor the strong ones. And a pear. We're
already getting pears from the succession houses."

"Ma'am, Miss Driscoll may not have any pears,"
Kinsford pointed out.

"No, then perhaps a rhubarb tart. Yes, I should
quite like that, or a gooseberry tart. Either will do."

Clarissa grinned at Meg and whispered, "Just
bring her anything we have, please. On a tray." She
cocked her head at Kinsford, raising her brows.

"No, I thank you. I'm not hungry," he said. William and Mr. Traling concurred.

Lady Kinsford held her daughter's uninjured hand
and sighed repeatedly. "The news reached me
through the servants. It would have been better if
you'd sent a message, Kinsford." Apparently the earl
had learned better than to respond.

Lady Kinsford was curious about Miss Driscoll's
house; fascinated, in fact, by the tiny size of the
room, as if it were a miniature, and she turned quite
around to see where the windows faced. Her eye
happened to fall next on Mr. Traling, who was doing
a pretty good job of keeping himself in the back-
ground. "I don't believe this gentleman is from the
area," Lady Kinsford commented.

"No, I'm from Bath," he said, bowing slightly to
her.

"I don't care for his being here when my daughter
lies insensate and unclothed," Lady Kinsford said.
"It's not seemly."

Clarissa wondered if by unclothed the countess
meant that Lady Aria's boots had been removed.
Only the very tips of her toes showed beneath the
blankets. Clarissa hastened to tuck them in.

Mr. Traling, however, was not proof against the
dowager's scowl; or he had finally determined that
there was no chance of his seeing Miss Driscoll alone
on this day. With a rueful grin, he handed Clarissa

the bottle of black draught, shrugged and said, "I'll be off then, Miss Driscoll. I certainly hope the young lady won't be any the worse for her fall." He bowed to the dowager, dipped his head to Kinsford and his brother, and mischievously squeezed Clarissa's hand as he shook it. Neither the earl nor his stepmama failed to notice this.

When he had left the room, the dowager suggested, "I believe you have a companion living with you, Miss Driscoll."

Without a moment's hesitation, Clarissa nodded. "Lorelia Snolgrass. She's not here at present. A very worthy woman, at the beck and call of her family. I believe it is her younger brother's wife who was in childbed and in great need of her. Undoubtedly she'll be back in a few weeks. So very exhausting, travel, don't you think?"

As Lady Kinsford never traveled anywhere, one might have thought she would agree with Miss Driscoll, but she merely sniffed and returned her attention to her daughter. Lady Aria was making feeble movements with her hands. Occasional low groans came from her throat. She tossed her head restlessly, dislodging the damp flannel.

"I'll get a warm one," Clarissa said, and left the four of them alone in the sitting room.

In the kitchen she found Meg preparing a tray of food for the dowager.

"Lady Aria may be pale now, ma'am," Meg said, "but in no time she could develop the fever. Shall I make up a fever-mixture?"

"Have we any carbonate of potash?"

"Enough for one receipt. I could get more later."

"Very well. Mr. Traling has brought us a bottle of black draught from Mrs. Luden."

"Oh, I feel certain we have some."

"It kept him busy and out of the way," Clarissa said tartly. "Though perhaps not long enough. I'll take another warm flannel in."

When she returned to open the sitting-room door, she overheard Lady Kinsford in full spate. "And I cannot believe that she would entertain a gentleman in the absence of her companion. Imagine! A single woman. A spinster in a small village."

"Usually I wear a cap," Clarissa pointed out as she came in. This did not discompose Lady Kinsford, but the earl looked acutely uncomfortable. "You must ask your stepson here. I was wearing one this morning. They're very effective, you know, in driving amorous intent out of young men. I swear by their efficacy myself, though I know others who champion the dragon companion. Not that Miss Snolgrass is a dragon, by any means."

She bent down to place the warm, moist flannel on Lady Aria's head. "Her color looks a little better, I think."

"We're grateful for your kind assistance," Kinsford assured her stiffly.

"Well, I've never seen her looking so pale," Lady Kinsford said. Then she frowned. "What were you doing here this morning, Kinsford?"

In a bland voice he replied, "Discussing Lady Aria's lessons with Miss Driscoll."

"That cannot have been at all necessary. *I* could have told you anything you needed to know." Though she awaited further explanation, he did not avail himself of the opportunity. After a very long time, which Clarissa would have described as a battle of wills, Lady Kinsford shrugged her shoulders. "Oh, very well. It's of no importance. It was your father, after all, who originally arranged the lessons, and Lady Aria is my daughter. I wouldn't have thought it was any of your concern.''

Clarissa had had enough of the discussion and would have stepped in to interrupt if Meg had not provided the necessary diversion. The maid came in with a tray loaded down in foodstuffs that Clarissa had forgotten were in the larder. There were two cheeses, a Cheshire and a Stilton; a cottage loaf of bread, sliced thin; several warm rolls; a lemon tart; and several pieces of fruit, though no pears.

"How lovely," Clarissa said, forestalling the dowager. "Perhaps Lady Kinsford would like to sit here at my desk to eat. It's so uncomfortable to eat from one's lap, don't you think, Lady Kinsford?"

"I wouldn't know," her visitor declared. "I've never done anything of the sort." But she obligingly made her regal way to the one bit of furniture which Clarissa truly loved and had salvaged from her father's estate. The little writing desk had inlaid marquetry and a dozen small drawers and cubbyholes for quills and accumulated letters and ink pots.

Meg set the tray on a table which she drew close to the desk and Lady Kinsford helped herself, frowning all the while. "No pears?" she asked.

"I'm afraid we had none, my lady," Meg replied.

"And it's a lemon tart, isn't it? I'm not particularly fond of lemon tart. But I shall eat it."

Gracious to the end, Clarissa thought with amusement. Kinsford offered a half-apologetic shrug and, to Clarissa's decided relief, made sure that the dowager's visit ended as soon as she had finished her repast.

4

Kinsford Hall was an imposing structure, dating originally from the sixteenth century. Additions had been undertaken by most of the Earls of Kinsford, some to good effect. The rough-hewn stone of the walls and battlements was contrasted by finely carved lighter stone for the window and door embrasures. There were finely carved stone chimneys with detailed chimney pots, all entirely too short to effectively remove smoke and reduce drafts.

The original interior of stone, stone, and more stone had given way to wood and plaster and rugs. Lady Kinsford's suite of rooms had actually been added by the fourth earl for his first wife, the present Lord Kinsford's mother. It was a charming, airy portion, with multitudinous windows and romantic flights of fancy in the ceiling decoration.

The present Lady Kinsford had added to the fanciful architecture her special touch of habit: She seldom left her suite. For that reason, Alexander Barrington, fifth Earl of Kinsford, presented himself there when she summoned him, though he would have preferred neutral territory. His stepmother's behavior at Miss Driscoll's had heightened his fears about her adequacy as guide to her own two children.

"Good evening, ma'am," he said as he took the seat she indicated. "I trust your excursion has not unduly tired you."

As Lady Kinsford was lying on a reclining chaise, with a cool cloth on her forehead, her wrists recently bathed in lavender water by her maid, this was spoken only as a pleasantry.

"I am as well as can be expected, Kinsford." She waved a hand in the direction of the village. "I think you made a mistake in allowing Aria to stay at that woman's house, Kinsford."

"I had little choice, and I'm sure she'll be perfectly fine. Miss Driscoll has known her for years and has explicit directions from the doctor as to her care."

"Aria said the doctor spoke of shaving her head. You don't think they would actually do that, do you?"

"No. Not unless it were totally unavoidable. You mustn't worry about such things, ma'am. Her hair would grow back in any case."

"But she's fifteen. This is not a time for her to be looking freakish." Lady Kinsford toyed with a lavender-scented handkerchief, pressing it briefly to the tip of her nose. "It was at fifteen when young men began to notice me. It's a precarious age for a girl. I should hate for her to suffer from this accident."

Kinsford felt a little impatient with the focus of her concern, but he forced himself to remain easy in the straight-backed chair to which she'd relegated him. "She's a healthy young thing," he said. "I'm sure she'll recover physically and mentally without any harm done." He was not unaware of the possibilities for damage, but he did not intend to alarm

Aria's mother with such worries. "Dr. Lawrence seemed satisfied with her condition."

"And what do you think of Miss Driscoll?" the dowager asked, peering up at him with a dubious frown.

"She strikes me as a trifle eccentric, but of no danger to the children. I promise you I will keep an eye on her."

"Then you're going to be around for a time?"

"Yes. A week or two at least." It was not what he'd planned, but there was nothing for it now but to stay. "Please don't distress yourself, ma'am. The situation is under control."

When he had escaped from his stepmother's overheated room, he sat for some time in his study considering what was best to be done. His brother, Will, had managed to avoid an encounter with him since the earl's return to Kinsford Hall and, since Will was the reason for Kinsford's coming, should doubtless be dealt with promptly.

The matter of the damaged field had only come to his attention through running into Mr. Olsen that morning. His subsequent discussion with Aria had prompted his visit to Miss Driscoll. Everything remained at loose ends. It was not a situation with which Kinsford was comfortable. *Something* needed to be settled definitively. He sent for Will.

But Will was not to be found. Kinsford left instructions that Will was to be brought to him at whatever hour he returned to the Hall, be it the middle of the night. He remained in his study, stretched out in his father's old leather chair, his feet up on the fender. There was a small fire against the chill of the early spring evening, and the flames glowed in his glass of brandy.

He was troubled by the realization that things had not proceeded smoothly at Kinsford Hall during his prolonged absence in London. If his estate manager, Mr. Alman, hadn't happened to write that Will was home from school, Kinsford would not have realized that any problem existed. Since it was school-term time, there was no satisfactory reason for Will being at Kinsford Hall. The necessity of coming into the country to investigate matters had sorely tried Kinsford's patience. He had work to do in London.

Four years previously, Kinsford had returned from his time in the army with Wellington dissatisfied with the way his country was being run. Though his father had seldom taken his seat in the House of Lords, Kinsford had decided to make his presence felt there. And to his own surprise, his energy and talents at politics had finally brought him into his own. He enjoyed the challenge of revitalizing a decaying system, the excitement of influencing men grown stuffy in their outmoded beliefs. In London, Kinsford knew he was having an effect on changing the very world in which he lived.

He took a sip of his brandy and set the glass down, frowning at the fire. Somehow changing the country seemed simple compared to controlling his half-brother and half-sister, paying attention to the problems his estate manager constantly placed before him, and bearing with his stepmother's fantasy world. Or, if not simpler, at least a great deal more interesting.

The earl hadn't the first idea how to handle a seventeen-year-old lad who belonged in school. He had, of course, once been seventeen himself. He remembered the time with a rather nostalgic affection. It was before he became a responsible, respected member of the community. How could he expect Will to do better than he had himself, especially when Will didn't have a father to act as a model?

Kinsford very much feared that he might have to stay in the country even longer than it would take Aria to get well. It was not a comfortable feeling. A rap on the door disturbed his reverie. "Come in."

Will stood uncertainly in the doorway. "You wanted to see me?"

"Yes. Come in and close the door." Kinsford rose and walked to the brandy decanter. "Would you like a glass?"

"No, thanks." At Kinsford's raised brow, he added, "I've just had a pint in Stanton Prior."

The earl poured himself a splash more and nodded to the chair opposite his. "We need to have a talk."

"Is Aria worse?"

"No, no. As far as I know, she's fine. I sent some pears over with Lucas this evening and Miss Driscoll reported that Aria was sleeping well and feeling a bit better."

"Good."

Though Kinsford stood for some time regarding his younger brother, Will was not discomfited into pouring out his heart. The earl remembered that he, too, had not been moved by such tactics, so he seated himself and asked, "Why are you home from school?"

"They sent me down for a prank. The head said he was sending Mama a letter about it."

"Your mother hasn't mentioned it."

"She doesn't always read her mail, Kinsford. Especially letters from people she don't know."

"I see." Kinsford could picture the letter stuffed somewhere in her desk, unopened. He sighed.

"Then you had best tell me yourself why you were sent down, and when you'll be allowed to return, if you will."

"Well, of course I shall be allowed to return, if I wish. I think, though, that I've had quite enough schooling for the time being, don't you?"

"I very much doubt it." Kinsford settled back in his chair. "Why were you sent down?"

"It was all on account of this silly gudgeon I'd taken to hanging about with. He simply could not keep a secret. Had to go and blab to everyone that we'd jammed the lock on the chapel. I mean, really, Kinsford, it's so cold in the chapel at that hour of the morning! You'd have thought they'd have a bit of a fire, wouldn't you?"

"I certainly don't remember them having one when I was there." Kinsford did remember shivering there many mornings of his youthful life. It had never occurred to him to jam the lock. "Was that all you did?"

Will considered the question for a moment, and apparently decided that honesty was the wisest course. "Dr. Winters, the head, you know, said it was the last straw. Not that I'd done anything so awful! We kidnapped one of the master's dogs because it was always biting fellows who ran down the path. We had no intention of hurting it or keeping it for more than a day or two. Just put a fright into the fellow so he'd keep the dog locked up, don't you see?"

"Yes, I see."

"And then," Will said, getting caught up in his recital, "there was the missing plum pudding. I wasn't responsible for that. Hurst was always up in the boughs about something and Upton took the pudding because Hurst had broken his favorite quizzing glass. So of course I ate it when it was offered to me, though it wasn't as good as all that. I fancy cook does a much better one.''

''Anything else?''

''Oh, just the usual stuff. You know. Roxie and I went into town one day for a lark. Weren't gone above three hours. I think it was Hurst who spilled the beans that time, too. Paltriest fellow, if you ask me.''

''And what's this I hear about the damage you and Aria did to Mr. Olsen's field?''

''Now who told you that?'' Will demanded. ''That was all settled long ago.''

''So I hear. And without your mother's or my knowledge.''

''Well, you weren't here, for heaven's sake,'' Will said reasonably. ''And it would have been useless to tell Mama because she wouldn't have seen the harm in it. She don't like Olsen above half.''

This concurrence with Aria's view of the situation merely served to heighten Kinsford's frustration. ''I don't quarrel with the way things have been arranged. It is the secrecy which distresses me.''

''You mean you wish you had known so you could comb my hair over it? Lord, Miss Driscoll did that well enough. You'd have thought we spent our time running down small children.''

It seemed a perfect opening for the other questions which were exercising his lordship. ''Why would Miss Driscoll concern herself in the matter at all? I realize she happened to be there, but it certainly was none of her concern.''

Will grinned. ''That's not the sort of thing that worries Miss Driscoll. For lack of anyone else,'' he admitted innocently, "she's taken on the duties of our moral arbiter. Sometimes, when we go for dancing lessons, she makes us consider social questions. Like, if we knew that Jim Hooper was out of work and had a wife and child to support, what would we do about it?"

"Who's Jim Hooper?"

"Oh, just a fellow over to Inglesbatch. Hardworking chap. Lost his job because the farmer there died and the property was sold."

Will shifted restlessly in his chair. "Well, I didn't see how it was my responsibility, and certainly not Aria's, but Miss Driscoll saw it quite differently. She said we were all our brother's keepers, and since we could with ease employ someone of Jim Hooper's skills, it was our duty to do so." His brows drew together. "I can't remember all her reasoning, but we talked to Alman and sure enough he gave Hooper a job. Worked out just fine and Miss Driscoll had Meg make us baked almond pudding to celebrate."

The story made Kinsford absolutely livid. He could not have said precisely why, and he attempted to conceal his anger from his brother. Only the tightening of the muscles in his jaw betrayed him. To distract Will he asked with patent disbelief, "How can Miss Driscoll teach you and Aria the latest dances when she hasn't any contact with society at all, stuck off here in Pennwick?"

"Damned if I know," Will admitted easily. "Seems to know just what's in fashion, though. Waltzes and quadrilles and such. She rather makes it fun for a fellow." He flushed. "Never thought I'd say that."

Chagrined, Kinsford took another tack. "Well, how about this companion of hers. Perhaps she's the one who teaches Miss Driscoll the dances. What's Miss Snolgrass like?''

"Never met her."

"You've never met her?" Kinsford was incredulous. "You've been going to Miss Driscoll for three years."

"Yes, but I'm more often away at school. Miss Snolgrass goes about a lot visiting family, you know. One time it's a sister, another an aunt. Very obliging woman, I dare say. She's even been to visit an old housekeeper in Surrey, and her governess (imagine!) in Wiltshire. Can't say I'd ever do that. Do you remember Miss Shreve? A termagant if ever there was one.''

Kinsford did not recall Miss Shreve, but that was beside the point. "Has your sister met Miss Snolgrass?''

"I expect so. It isn't the sort of thing we discuss, Kinsford. I mean, the woman is a companion. Probably a mousy sort of person who hasn't a thing to say for herself.''

"Are you certain," the earl asked sternly, "that Miss Snolgrass exists?''

Will blinked at him. "Well, of course she exists, gudgeon. She's Miss Driscoll's companion.''

"But no one has ever seen her."

"Lots of people have seen her," Will protested. "Ask anyone in the village.''

"Very well. But she can't be much of a companion if she's never there.''

"How much of a companion does Miss Driscoll need?" Will asked, with a wave of his eager young hands. "She has a maid and she never goes anywhere out of the village. I dare say she only has Miss

Snolgrass to live with her because the woman has nowhere else to go."

"A young woman of Miss Driscoll's age cannot live alone," Kinsford reminded him.

"Young?" Will laughed. "She's almost as old as you are, Kinsford. And she wears those silly white caps all the time. She doesn't ride or drive or go about to entertainments except in the immediate neighborhood. Why should she need to have someone always with her?"

"It's what's done."

"A sterling reason," Will retorted.

"Her reputation could be damaged if she didn't abide by such social rules."

"What reputation? Miss Driscoll is just Miss Driscoll. Everyone here knows her, and has known her since she was born. Poor soul has come down so in the world, it would be just like a bunch of old biddies to make sport of her. But I wouldn't expect it of you, Kinsford."

"I'm not making sport of her," his brother insisted. "I'm simply pointing out the delicacy of her position. What about this man who came to visit her?"

"You see!" Will jumped up from his chair and stalked around the room, stopping in front of the fire. "That's the sort of thing I wouldn't even expect of Lady Herbert."

Sir John Herbert owned the manor house to the south of Pennwick village. His lady was a delightful and kind woman, but an inveterate gossip. Lord Kinsford did not relish being compared with her. "I'm not suggested there's anything improper going on," he said. "With her companion present the subject would simply not arise."

"It needn't arise if her companion is away, either."

"Don't fly into a miff." Kinsford draped one buckskin-clad leg over the other and leaned back in his chair in an effort to convince his brother that he was perfectly at ease himself. "I'm curious. I've never met Mr. Traling before. I gather he's from Bath."

Will shrugged. "I'm sure I don't know. I've only seen him once or twice before."

"At Miss Driscoll's?"

Will glared at him. "There you go again, insinuating that there's something amiss with him being there. Miss Driscoll isn't that sort of woman, Kinsford. And I've never seen him there except in the morning. Perfectly normal thing, a morning visit."

"Does her maid live in?"

Will stalked to the door. "I'm not going to answer any more of your shabby questions. She's one of the nicest people I've ever met and I won't be a party to such innuendo."

"I'm not suggesting anything improper," Kinsford protested again, but the door had already snapped sharply shut behind William. At another time Kinsford might have gone after him. Tonight he was too uncertain of his temper to do so. It seemed perfectly likely to him that he was indeed maligning Miss Driscoll's character by suggestion, because he felt almost unbearably annoyed with her.

Imagine her setting herself up as character-builder to his brother and sister. As if he weren't capable of such a task! It didn't matter just then that he was seldom at home; Will and Aria were supposed to absorb sterling characteristics from him at whatever distance he maintained.

And it irritated him beyond bearing that Aria was at that moment in Miss Driscoll's house, being taken care of by someone who was not even family: a woman whose father had gambled away his estate, leaving his daughter with so little she could only afford a cottage and a single servant. It was not the life to which she had been born and bred, making a living teaching pianoforte, drawing, and dancing to the neighborhood gentry.

Not that the Barringtons had any reason to reproach themselves for their treatment of her. His father, the fourth earl, had gone so far as to purchase the manor house at a very reasonable price to make it possible for Miss Driscoll to satisfy her father's debts. And, though she'd refused the offer, he'd suggested that Miss Driscoll remain at Pennhurst for an indefinite time.

The fact that the fourth earl had been one of Mr. Driscoll's major creditors was totally irrelevant.

5

Early morning sun streamed through the windows of the dining parlor and fell on the polished mahogany table. Clarissa had finished her muffin but not the cold veal-and-ham pie. Her attention had wandered and she stared unseeing at a vine swaying across the multipaned window, a thin, veiny vine with no flowers but fresh green leaves. Clarissa barely noticed it, her mind was so locked in the past, on an event that she had managed to push out of her thoughts so long ago it seemed almost a dream. Perhaps it *was* a dream. A girlish daydream she had had when she lived at Pennhurst.

She was climbing over a stile, dressed in one of those delightful walking dresses she had worn then, of thin jaconet muslin over a pale peach-colored sarsenet slip, a triple fall of lace at the throat. Like spring personified, she had radiated freshness and youth and unfurling potential. The last of a group of young people to make her way over the stile, she was being handed down by the young man in front of her, Alexander Barrington.

He was not then yet earl, of course, but a rather wild young man. He went where he liked; he did what he chose. And he chose then to kiss her. Clarissa had never been kissed, and as kisses go, it was not much of a kiss. But his eyes had sparkled with mischief and he'd held her hands in both of his as she hopped to the ground. Then, so quickly she could not be sure later that she hadn't dreamed it, he'd brushed his lips against hers, and murmured, "Goddess of spring."

There had never been any acknowledgment of this moment, by either of them. For some time Clarissa had treasured it, thinking that perhaps it meant the young Viscount Barrington was interested in her. Not that she would have welcomed attention from such a reckless, feckless fellow, though there was no denying that he had been an exciting man. But he had given the neighborhood females a wide berth, and soon had left the country altogether to take up his military career.

Her reverie was shattered by a jaunty knock on the front door. She started somewhat guiltily, pushing the memory from her again. Aria was still asleep in the sitting room, but there was much to be attended to.

Meg stuck her head around the door. "Are you at home, Miss Driscoll?"

"I don't see how I can avoid it," she replied tartly. "Bring whoever it is in here first. And perhaps you'd better bring more tea and muffins."

In a moment Meg returned to announce William. Clarissa sighed her relief and rose smiling at him. "Your sister is still sleeping, William. Join me for a cup of tea."

"Does she seem all right, Miss Driscoll? I'm worried about concussion. They say it's very dangerous." He took the seat she offered and looked about for a cup. When he didn't find one, he shrugged. "I've had breakfast."

"Meg will bring what you need." Clarissa tucked a wandering strand of hair under her lace cap. "Lady Aria seems to be resting comfortably. If she's hungry when she awakens, it will be a good sign, the doctor said."

"She's always hungry," Will assured her, before realizing that she had always, previously, been well. He stared forlornly at the vase in the center of the table which held tulips and daffodils. "I suppose if she were at home we'd have flowers in her room. She's very fond of them. I'll have some sent over."

"Thank you. I hope your mama is not too worried."

Meg brought in a fresh pot of tea with a basket of muffins. From the corner cabinet she retrieved a cup and saucer and a matching plate which she set in front of William. Forgetting that he had intended to skip this second meal, he spread marmalade on a toasted muffin.

"It's hard to say with Mama. She isn't very realistic, you see. Sometimes she worries about us when there's not a thing in the world to warrant it, and sometimes she does not when there's something quite serious. I think she has determined that Aria will be perfectly fine, and as she's not at the Hall to remind Mama that she is indisposed, Mama may be able to completely ignore the problem."

Clarissa was a little taken aback by this succinct description of Lady Kinsford's mental processes. "She must know she is welcome any time to visit with Lady Aria. As you all are, of course."

Will grinned. "I can hardly wait to see everyone here again, like yesterday. Lord, that was a rare treat! You should have heard Kinsford last night." He stopped abruptly, remembering that Miss Driscoll was not exactly the person to be telling about his brother's suspicions. He hastened to add, "Firebird was perfectly all right, fortunately. Not a scratch on her and not the least nervous, either, when we found her in the south meadow. As a rule she's rather high-strung. Do you never ride, Miss Driscoll?"

Clarissa would have liked to quiz him on Kinsford's pique, but she could see it would embarrass William and she refrained. "I haven't ridden in years. It's far too expensive to keep a horse. But I rode when I was your age."

"Of course you did." He ran a hand through his already disordered blond locks. "How thoughtless we've been. You must send for a horse from the Hall anytime you wish to ride. No, more than that. When Aria is up and about again, we shall all ride together."

"That's very kind of you," Clarissa said dismissively. "Why don't I check on your sister now? She may be awake."

When he rose with her, she merely waved him back to his seat. No sense having him tag along at her heels like a puppy. She shut the door behind her when she went quietly into the sitting room. Aria was lying on the sofa with the blankets about her, but her eyes were open. She regarded Clarissa quizzically.

"I remember having a fall, and seeing Dr. Lawrence here, but I'm not sure why I'm not at home," she said.

"They thought it best not to move you for a while. Your shoulder was dislocated, and you had a pretty bad blow to the head. How do you feel?"

Aria wrinkled her nose. "Not very well. My head aches abominably."

"I'm not surprised. Meg has been putting compresses on your temple. I'll see if she has another one ready." Clarissa felt Aria's forehead as she spoke. The fever which had come on some hours after the fall was abating now, but she would need to administer another fever pill, according to Dr. Lawrence's instructions. "Are you hungry, Lady Aria?"

"A little."

"Meg could make you some barley gruel." Clarissa fluffed the pillow under Aria's head. "Do you think you'd like that?"

"Yes, if she stirs in a little jam. That's the way I liked it as a child."

"Fine. Your brother is here, my dear. Shall I send him in?"

Aria frowned. "I'm not really up to being scolded, Miss Driscoll. Could you tell him I'm not well enough to see him?"

"I didn't mean Lord Kinsford. It's William who's in the dining parlor."

"Well, of course Will shall come in. My word, is it that late in the morning? Your clock says only nine."

"The clock is correct."

Aria's eyes widened. "And Will is here already? He must be very concerned about me to get up at this hour."

"I'm sure he is." Clarissa turned to leave but decided there was something more she needed to say. "Everyone is concerned about you, Lady Aria. Your mother hurried here yesterday and Lord Kinsford made sure you had the best care available. You needn't fear that Lord Kinsford will scold you."

"Little you know," Aria scoffed as she leaned back against the pillow. "He means well but he doesn't know how to talk to us without scolding, or teaching us a lesson, or ordering us to do something.''

"Then we'll have to instruct him, won't we?" Clarissa said in her most tutorial voice, a faint smile tugging at her lips. "For you know he's going to insist on seeing you."

Aria pulled the pillow over her face. "Tell him I've expired, why don't you?"

"I'll send William in."

When Clarissa returned with the gruel, she found brother and sister chattering away about the state of the Kinsford Hall stables with Kinsford's return. He had apparently brought not only Longbridge, but the chestnut pair that drew his curricle to admiration. When she set the gruel on a table for Aria, Will said, "Is that all she gets? Mush?"

"It's gruel and it's what I asked for," Aria told him. "Don't be rude, Will."

He moaned. "She's worse than I thought, isn't she, Miss Driscoll? Else why would she want such stuff?"

"Because it's easy to digest and very soothing," Clarissa informed him. "Why don't you run along now so she can eat in peace? Come back this afternoon."

"Oh, very well." he pressed his sister's fingers as he rose to leave. "Don't let Kinsford bother you. He's in one of his pets."

"There, I knew it," Aria said when he had disappeared. "I don't want to see Alexander, Miss Driscoll. If he comes, you are to say I'm fast asleep."

"We'll see."

Aria glared at her. "Promise me! It's not fair to

be sick and have to bear his teasing me with his fidgets. I won't see him!'' Her cheeks became flushed and her eyes glittered with the possibility of tears.

"Very well. We'll discuss it later. Right now I hope you'll have your gruel and the tea Meg made you. And there are some French plums in the box, if you wish them."

Aria sighed as Clarissa put a tray across her legs, but she immediately picked up the spoon and tried the gruel. "Oh, good, she's done it with raspberry jam, my favorite. Thank you, Miss Driscoll."

There was an imperative knock at the door. Aria paused briefly, the spoon halfway to her mouth. "Remember," she said urgently. "I'm asleep."

Clarissa nodded and left the room.

Kinsford hadn't seen his brother Will that morning, so he had been unable to invite him along on his visit to Aria, which he had wanted to do in an effort to smooth things out between them. Lady Kinsford had made Kinsford the bearer of a note to her daughter, for which he'd had to wait a full half hour.

He tied Longbridge outside the cottage, expecting a moderate stay, but not one long enough to have one of the village children walk the horse. It wouldn't due to overtire his sister.

Meg opened the door to him and invited him into the small hall, but before she could go for her mistress, Miss Driscoll appeared from the sitting room. She closed the door carefully behind her, and put her finger to her lips, motioning him to follow her into the dining parlor. While Meg returned to the rear of the house, Kinsford followed Miss Driscoll.

"I had hoped to see Aria," he said immediately, removing his riding gauntlets and holding them in one hand. "How does she go on?"

"She's much better this morning, but her head still aches abominably and she's drifted off to sleep again. It would be unfair to awaken her, when she has such discomfort."

Kinsford could not tell whether Miss Driscoll was lying to him or not. "Perhaps she'll awaken again soon. I could sit quietly in the sitting room . . ."

Miss Driscoll bristled. "I'm afraid not. Lady Aria needs all the rest she can get. If you need reassurance as to her condition, you should apply to your brother. He was here when she was awake."

"Will got to see her?" Kinsford felt seriously put out. He suspected that Miss Driscoll was *not* telling him the truth, though it would serve no purpose for her to prevent him from seeing his sister. Therefore, he suspected that Will had somehow urged her to keep him away from Aria, and he would not tolerate that. "I believe as head of the family that I should ascertain for myself what her condition is this morning. So, begging your pardon, I shall just look in on her."

"You will do no such thing!" Miss Driscoll flushed with indignation. "This is *my* house, Lord Kinsford, and I am in charge of your sister while she's here. If you wish to have her removed to the Hall against Dr. Lawrence's orders, that is of course your concern. I would strongly advise against it, but I cannot prevent you from doing so. In the meantime, you will behave according to my wishes in my house."

Kinsford had not been spoken to in such a way since his father was alive. If he had been seriously put out before, he was now furious. It would not, however, serve the least purpose to allow this impertinent young woman to see his fury.

Apparently his attempt at masking his emotions was unsuccessful, for she said, "Yes, yes, I'm sure I will understand that you couldn't possibly allow the young ones to take lessons from me after this. And I didn't say that you couldn't see your sister while she's here. Will has seen her. When she's ready to see you, you can see her, too."

"What do you mean, 'when she's ready' to see me?" he demanded, his eyes narrowing.

"When she's awake and feeling up to company, you may certainly visit with her. In the meantime, you will probably wish to leave that missive with me to give her after you leave."

Kinsford had forgotten the sheet of paper he held. He would as soon have burned it as given it into her care, but he handed it over, turned on his heel, and strode out of the dining parlor into the hall. There he hesitated for the merest fraction of a second, and Miss Driscoll, following close behind him, said, "You will remember what the doctor said. We are to watch for disorientation, not cause it, Lord Kinsford." Disgruntled, since he had not seriously thought of entering the sitting room, he let himself out the front door.

But the more he thought of it afterward, the more convinced he became that Aria had been awake. Since it did not occur to him that his sister might not have wished to see him, he was convinced that either Miss Driscoll or Will had determined that he should not be allowed access to his sister.

He swung onto Longbridge, nudged his horse forward, and soon found himself at the edge of town facing the same road he and Aria had taken the previous day. In the very short time since he'd returned to Kinsford Hall, he had managed to alienate both his sister and his brother, and to become mightily enraged with their dancing instructor. Though Kinsford was not in the habit of questioning himself, it did just impinge on his consciousness that there might be something wrong with this scenario, and that it might have something to do with him.

Lady Aria had indeed been awake when her brother was present in the house. Though she could not hear what Miss Driscoll and he had discussed in the dining parlor, she had recognized from the timbre of their voices that they were arguing. Though grateful to Miss Driscoll for preserving her from her brother's homilies, she felt she had pushed things in the wrong direction. She wanted Alexander to like Miss Driscoll, not be annoyed with her.

Her head, though it ached considerably, was quite clear. And Aria was a very resourceful young woman, sick or not. It seemed to her that the longer she remained in Miss Driscoll's house, the better chance there was for these two important people in her life to get to know one another. Surely they could not help but respect each other once they had established that kind of familiarity.

Aria had caught Miss Driscoll's remark in the hall about disorientation, which gave her a splendid idea. They wouldn't move her to the Hall if she had such a problem, would they?

Clarissa returned to the dining parlor after the door closed behind the earl. It was not her habit to antagonize anyone, and certainly not the local aristocracy. But her cheeks flushed when she remembered him telling her that he was going to check on his sister in spite of what she'd said. Apparently it was not enough for the Barringtons to own her father's manor house; now they were intent on trespassing in her own small cottage. Well, she would not tolerate that, even if it meant the end of the greater part of her very limited income. She would open a village school before she would allow the Earl of Kinsford to dictate to her what he intended to do in her own house.

When another knock came at the door, she was strongly disposed to tell Meg to ignore it. She was not in the mood to handle any more Barringtons. But it was only a neighbor bringing calves' foot jelly for the invalid, someone who wished only to be helpful. When the woman had gone, Clarissa wandered to the sitting room and found Aria indeed sound asleep.

The girl looked quite beautiful lying there with her hand tucked up under her cheek. The swelling on her head had come down considerably. No danger now of having to shave an area to rub in Dr. Lawrence's lotion. Clarissa tucked the covers gently around the resting child and decided she'd best take her constitutional now before anyone else arrived.

Giving strict instructions to Meg that no one was to disturb the girl while she slept, Clarissa donned her blue pelisse and cottage bonnet. If she'd had to give up riding when the manor was sold, she had discovered the pleasures of walking to compensate. On a bright spring day such as this she could walk for hours.

6

Steven Traling was three-and-twenty, and usually full of boyish enthusiasm and spirits. His brown eyes frequently danced and his black hair did not always fall perfectly into the prevailing Brutus style. He was not above average height and he rode well, if not brilliantly. It was his habit to come to Pennwick every two weeks or so, but as he had not had a chance to be private with Miss Driscoll the previous day, he returned to Pennwick. He was riding his horse along the main street (if such the rutted lane could be called) of the village when he spied Miss Driscoll striding off across the fields at the end of town.

He thought her a magnificent figure of a woman. Though he was aware that she walked constantly for her own amusement (he had had to wait on numerous occasions for her return), he had not actually watched her stride across a field with that air of certainty with which she did everything. Unlike his wife, who was a beautiful but timid woman.

Mr. Traling rode his horse to the end of the lane, dismounted and tied him to a tree. He was able to overtake Miss Driscoll in a matter of minutes, despite her ambitious pace. "Good morning, Miss Driscoll," he called with engaging formality when he was close enough.

Surprised, Clarissa swung around to confront him. "Mr. Traling. What are you doing in Pennwick today?"

"Yesterday was hardly a satisfactory visit, was it?" he asked. "Never saw so many people in such a small space in my life. Hope the girl's mending all right."

"She seems to be. She's staying with me for a few days, as it would have been risky to transfer her to the Hall in her condition."

Traling grinned. "I imagine the family loved that!"

"Not in the least," Clarissa admitted. "But they had little choice." She returned to her former pace and he matched his stride with hers. "How did you manage to elude your in-laws two days in a row?"

"It wasn't easy. Mrs. Wilton decided to take Jane shopping for swaddling gowns or some such thing, but Mr. Wilton wished me to accompany him to the Pump Room. Odious place. Bath is so full of quizzes and they simply cannot wait to get their hands on a bit of gossip. I told Mr. Wilton the newest rumor was that Wellington was emigrating to the United States and it made him so mad he refused to go."

Clarissa couldn't restrain a gurgle of laughter. "Wellington in America! You have the most fertile imagination, Steven."

"I wish he would go!" the young man declared. "Perhaps my papa-in-law would join him there."

"And you would end up in America as well," she pointed out.

"Oh, I'm not so sure. I could probably convince Jane that she didn't want to go. Then they would be there and we would be here, a much more suitable arrangement than the current one.''

They had reached a path which led through a small coppice of copper beeches. Clarissa turned onto the path and headed west on the second leg of the triangle she sometimes made on her walks. Mr. Traling kept pace with her, frowning slightly as he considered his situation. "It wouldn't be so bad if they didn't put so much store in the baby," he remarked. "Poor Jane can't make a move without her mother saying, 'You mustn't tire yourself, Jane,' or her father saying, 'Let's make sure this is a healthy lad, Jane.' What if it's not the son they expect? Or what if it's sickly and dies? You know that can happen.''

"Jane is their only child. Of course they're concerned."

"Oh, it's more than that. You know it is."

Clarissa sighed. "Yes. They're just naturally overbearing people who insist on controlling everything that concerns their daughter. You knew that when you married her, Steven.''

She only called him by his Christian name when there was no one else around. Right now they were in the middle of Priory Lane, fresh greenery springing out on either side, with a sweep of fields all about them. Far away to the north could be seen some of the spires of Bath itself; straight ahead lay Stanton Prior. At the hedgerow they would turn back toward the village of Pennwick.

Grudgingly, he admitted that he had known what his in-laws were when he married. "But, you know," he said, kicking a stone out of his path, "Jane didn't seem so cowed by them then. I think I depended more on her being a stronger person.''

Clarissa regarded him with assessing eyes. "Perhaps you expected that *you* would be a stronger person, Steven. Or thought you would have more power when you were actually married."

"And so I should have," he agreed, with asperity. "Under the marriage settlement I was to have control of her fortune. How was I to know that her father still controlled the source of funds? I'm not an attorney. And God knows I couldn't have afforded one to go over the settlement. It *sounded* perfectly all right."

"You'll come about. Just be patient. Once the baby is born and Jane settles into motherhood, she may very well side with you in having a home of your own—at some distance from your in-laws."

"Faint hope."

As Mr. Traling was seldom this despondent, in fact was almost never anything less than charming and cheerful, Clarissa was about to test him further on the cause of his black humor, when they were interrupted by a rider on the road. This was unfortunate, because Clarissa never went about with Mr. Traling. Though he came to her house once a fortnight or so, they never went into the village or about the neighborhood. It was a simple matter of prudence. There was wont to be talk in a small village. Clarissa was not one to explain herself or her actions, but neither was she in the habit of provoking her neighbors to talk about her. The rider, on closer approach, turned out to be William.

"Miss Driscoll! Mr. Traling." William tipped his hat to them. "Glad you could get out walking. I was afraid having Aria in the house would just about lock you in."

"She's sleeping now, and Meg is there to take care

of any of her needs." Clarissa frowned. "I've just remembered the doctor, though. I should like to be there when he calls."

"Not likely to miss him in the morning. Sees the more urgent cases then."

"Goodness. How do you know that?"

"Well, he told me yesterday when I went to get him, don't you know? Good sort of man. Very comfortable." William dismounted from his horse and led it as they walked. He didn't notice the look of exasperation Mr. Traling gave him. "Must be rather unnerving to be a doctor. Don't know what you'll find when you get to the scene of an accident, and everyone there expecting you to make everything right again."

Clarissa agreed with him, and Mr. Traling grunted. The rest of the way back to Clarissa's cottage, the three of them discussed the potential hazards of being a doctor as they walked. William had obviously given the matter a certain amount of thought overnight. "Have you ever noticed," he asked, "that doctors are the sort of people who are never surprised? I imagine they've seen everything. And another thing: not the sort of profession younger sons go into, is it? I mean, there's the church and the law and the military. Do all those things, but never medicine. I wonder why that is? Gets one's hands too dirty?"

"I believe that must be it," Mr. Traling said, taking part in the conversation for the first time. "Had you been considering becoming a doctor, William?"

"Me?" The young man considered him with astonishment. "I don't even know how to wrap one of those things around a horse's knees when they're swollen. And I'm as like as not to pass out at the sight of blood.''

"I merely wondered at your interest," Mr. Traling explained. "I didn't mean to suggest that you were planning on entering *any* profession."

William stared thoughtfully down the village lane to the fields beyond. "Do you think I should, Miss Driscoll?" he asked suddenly. "Study for a profession, I mean. Not become a doctor. Somehow I can't think Kinsford would approve of that. And I've never done very well at school, you know. More a matter of not applying myself than not having the native ability, I've always assumed, but who is to know?"

Clarissa, already in sufficient trouble with the earl, bowed out of this discussion. "I'm sure I haven't the least notion what would be best for you, William. This is the sort of thing you have to think about and talk over with your brother and your mother."

"My mother!" Now William regarded her with astonishment. "What would my mother have to say to such a scheme? She wouldn't understand in the least what I was about."

"I'm not at all sure I do either," Clarissa confessed. "Don't you enjoy being a gentleman of leisure?"

"Yes, well, of course I do. I shouldn't like at all to have to be at someone's beck and call, you know. But Kinsford went into the military when he was little older than I am, and perhaps I should do the same."

"There's not a great call for military personnel just now," Mr. Traling informed him. "What with old Boney out of the way and all. Pretty quiet on that front."

William nodded. "Suppose it is, at that. Well, it was only a thought. Mr. Traling, I'll ride with you to the Bath Road. I have an errand at the Whittaker farm."

Mr. Traling, who had hoped for a few words alone with Miss Driscoll, reluctantly agreed. He was not, apparently, destined to have further private time with her. She was impatient now to check on her young charge, he could tell. So he and William swung up on their horses and made their farewells. Clarissa, with a furrowed brow, watched them leave.

There was something very odd about the way William had acted, but she could not put her finger on it. He was, after all, a rather exuberant young man and one never quite knew where his thoughts would take him. But a profession! Lord have mercy on us, she thought, as, shaking her head, she entered the cottage.

Lady Aria was awake, and rather feverish. She shifted restlessly on the sofa, saying little but looking flushed and in pain. When questioned, she admitted that it was her head that ached. The wounded area remained swollen, but not nearly so much so as the previous day. Still, Clarissa determined that they should indeed rub in some lotion, as the doctor had suggested.

Meg left to make up the solution of sal ammoniac, vinegar, and whisky in water. Clarissa sat down with her charge, taking the warm hand in both of hers. "Poor dear. You must be miserable. But I have just been with your brother William and will divert you with his latest start."

Her patient turned interested but pained eyes to her and Clarissa continued, "He is considering whether he should take up a profession!"

Lady Aria giggled. "Will? How absurd he is. Whatever put that start in his mind?"

"I think it must have been his dealings with Dr. Lawrence yesterday."

"Will wants to be a doctor?" she asked, incredulous.

"Oh, no. Apparently that is far too lowly a profession for a gentleman. Something like the military seems more to his taste."

"He would look splendid in a uniform, but I cannot believe he would like it at all—the orders and the miserable conditions."

"Mr. Traling thought there was not a great deal of demand for military officers just now," Clarissa said.

Lady Aria turned her head fretfully on the pillow. "I suppose not, and I'm glad. I should hate for Will to go off and become a soldier."

Clarissa wished to keep her patient awake long enough to apply the lotion, so she asked, "Do you think William needs some form of occupation? Being down from school he may well be at loose ends."

Lady Aria's shrug sent a different sort of pain through her body and she gasped. Clarissa continued to stroke her hand. In a moment the added discomfort ceased and Aria attempted to answer Miss Driscoll's question. "He's always found plenty to do before this: hunting, fishing, riding, driving, going to the races, training his dogs. It's probably just some notion he's taken because Alexander has been plaguing him."

"We should talk about Lord Kinsford," Clarissa began. But at that moment Meg brought in the lotion and Lady Aria grimaced when Clarissa applied it liberally through her hair. It was a painful process and when she was finished, she patted the girl's good shoulder and said, "Why don't you try to get some sleep now, my dear? You'll feel better if you do."

Without a word Aria sank into a light, uneasy sleep and Clarissa tucked the covers about her carefully before leaving the room. Meg had a nuncheon laid out for her on the table in the dining parlor. After her walk, Clarissa had a good appetite, but she was distracted by her concern for the girl. What if Lady Aria had indeed sustained damage to her head, to her brain? She seemed perfectly coherent, though feverish and sleepy. Would they be able to tell at this point? Her shoulder was a minor matter. It would heal quickly. But her head . . . The more she pondered the matter, the more Clarissa grew eager for the doctor's visit.

When Dr. Lawrence arrived, however, he was accompanied by Lord Kinsford. Clarissa suspected that Lord Kinsford had skulked about at the edge of the village awaiting the doctor's arrival, only to "happen" to fall in with him there and gain admittance along with him to his sister's sickroom. As though Clarissa had intended to deny him access to his sister for the duration of her stay! Clarissa shrugged off the episode. Lady Aria was her first concern.

She led the way into the sitting room, where the young woman was still sleeping, her cheeks flushed. Dr. Lawrence took her wrist and felt her pulse. Lady Aria came only sightly awake at the movement. Her eyes seemed not to focus right away on the doctor and she frowned. "What is it?" she asked.

"It's Dr. Lawrence, Lady Aria," he said, touching her forehead and then her shoulder. "Do you remember where you are?"

"At Miss Driscoll's."

"And do you remember why?"

"I've had a fall from my horse."

"Good. Do you know when that happened?"

"I'm not sure," she said, her voice low and uncertain.

"Right. Don't be concerned. You've been sleeping off and on so that what day it is mightn't be quite clear." Dr. Lawrence leaned over to open his black bag. "I'm going to examine her now, Lord Kinsford. If you would wait in the hall."

Kinsford reluctantly let himself out into the hall and Clarissa heard Meg offer him a cup of tea in the dining parlor. She heard their footsteps retreat to the next room.

Dr. Lawrence proceeded to examine his patient, listening to her chest, palpating her abdomen, checking her wrists and ankles, adjusting the bandages about her relocated shoulder. Lady Aria said very little, responding only to direct questions, and then with monosyllabic answers. Dr. Lawrence spent a long time looking in her eyes and checking her scalp.

"You've put some lotion on?" he asked.

"Yes. Her head had been aching intolerably," Clarissa explained.

"It would be better to shave off a little of the hair, but I won't insist upon it. I know how awkward it is for a young lady. Still, you must attempt to get as much lotion on as possible. Several times a day. Every few hours, if you can manage it."

"Certainly we can manage."

He sighed, stepping away from the sick bed and lowering his voice. "It's hard to tell if there's anything seriously amiss. We'll need to keep a close watch on her for the next few days. I wouldn't move her. Not even upstairs, if you can handle the disruption of your household."

"It's no problem at all," Clarissa assured him. "I wonder if you would tell Lord Kinsford exactly the same thing. I very much fear he'll suggest moving her."

Dr. Lawrence regarded her thoughtfully. "I can't see why he should, and it would be most unwise. In fact, it wouldn't be a good idea to distress Lady Aria in any way at this juncture. I'll have a word with him."

"Thank you."

He walked back to Lady Aria and assured her that he would return the next day, sooner if she needed him. He had a comforting way about him, as William had remarked. Confident, competent—just the sort of doctor Clarissa would have wished for her charge.

She stayed with her patient when the doctor left the room. There was already a chair drawn up to the side of the sofa and she seated herself there to rub more lotion onto Lady Aria's wound. Though it stung momentarily, the girl relaxed when Clarissa continued to massage her temples. Within minutes she had fallen asleep again.

The door opened quietly and Kinsford stood for a few moments regarding the scene. Clarissa met his eyes with a steady gaze. She couldn't tell precisely what he was thinking, but his frustration was apparent.

"I'll return this evening," he whispered. And then, as an afterthought, "If I may."

"She'll probably be asleep."

"I won't disturb her."

"Very well."

7

Clarissa checked on Lady Aria frequently over the next few hours. Her fever seemed about the same, neither reducing significantly nor elevating alarmingly. She was a little less fretful in her sleep, perhaps, and her sleep remained unbroken, since no more visitors insisted on seeing her for the rest of the afternoon.

Keeping country hours, Clarissa ate her evening meal early and then returned to the sitting room. Aria was awake and slightly confused. "Where are my watercolors?" she asked, looking about the familiar room. "I shan't be able to draw without them. I want to paint the ha-ha behind the Hall. Will was chasing a fox cub and I especially wanted to paint him."

Disorientation being one of the signs Dr. Lawrence had particularly cautioned her about, Clarissa felt a start of alarm. She seated herself beside the sofa and laid a hand on Aria's forehead. It was no warmer. "You've not been well, my dear. We'll save the watercolors for later."

"Oh, yes," Aria agreed, blinking up at her. "How stupid of me!"

As she had herself awoken from vivid dreams that lingered, Clarissa could not determine whether this constituted disorientation. When Aria declared that she was hungry, Clarissa took it as a very good sign indeed and rang for Meg.

"Could you tolerate a toasted muffin? Or more gruel?"

"A muffin, please. And an orange, if you have one."

Very promising, Clarissa thought. But when the muffin was brought, Lady Aria's appetite had somewhat abandoned her. She took a bite and then lay back on the sofa, uninterested in anything further. Meg took the toasted muffin away, but left the orange to tempt their charge a little later. Clarissa asked if Lady Aria would like her to read to her a little, and the girl smiled.

"Just as if I were a child again," she said, but happily. "I should like that very much. Have you a copy of *Evelina*?"

Clarissa laughed. "Of course. What would a household be without a copy of *Evelina*?" And for the next hour she read to her patient, who seemed to follow the story with no difficulty, if possibly not quite the total interest that she might have on another occasion. They were about to begin another chapter when there was a knock at the front door of the cottage. Clarissa hadn't the least doubt as to who it would be. She tried to prepare Lady Aria.

"That will be the earl. He's very concerned about you and said he would be back this evening to check." At Aria's frown, she added, "I cannot very well keep him from you, my dear. He's your brother and your guardian. I promise you he will not upset you. That's not the least bit his intention."

"It is never his *intention*," Lady Aria said. "And yet he invariably manages to do so."

"Lord Kinsford," Meg announced, stepping back to allow the earl to enter.

He was dressed rather handsomely, in a coat of blue superfine, and wearing pantaloons that fit his athletic legs very well. On him the Barrington chin looked more determined than aristocratic, though it was likely that with age it would soften. His brown hair was well cut, obviously by a London barber. His neckcloth was modestly but elegantly tied. He was, in fact, a rather striking figure of a man, the one disconcerting element being his eyes. While they were a rich deep blue and well placed under heavy brows, they were the most assessing eyes Clarissa could ever remember seeing. No wonder the children thought them judgmental.

"Miss Driscoll, Aria." His acknowledging nod was cordial, as if he were determined to make a better start this time. He turned to his sister to ask, "How do you go on this evening, Aria? Your mother has sent another epistle and wishes a full report of you."

His sister took the letter he extended, and tucked it down under the sofa pillow as she had done with the other. Clarissa was not sure whether Aria had remembered to read the last one, and if the same fate were likely for this most recent one.

"I'm a little better," Aria assured him stoutly. "My head still aches, but not so much, I think. And my shoulder is a great deal less sore than it was. My fever makes me feel a little odd, but that will go away."

"Odd? How so?" The earl placed a hand on her forehead to feel her temperature. A small frown appeared on his brow. "You're still quite warm. Have you taken the fever draught?"

Clarissa answered for her patient, since she wasn't sure Aria would remember. "Every four hours today, according to Dr. Lawrence's instructions."

"And the wound?" He held Aria's chin with his fingers and turned her head so he could better see it. The light was failing outside, however, and he turned to Miss Driscoll. "If I might have a candle, ma'am."

There was a candleholder with candle and flint nearby on the table near the window. Clarissa felt vaguely annoyed with him for his request, but granted mentally that it was just. She struck the flint and when the paper flared she lit the candle. Instantly it threw light and shadows around the room that made it feel less familiar, almost mysterious. How very fanciful of me, Clarissa thought as she held the light up for the earl to see. His face took on a rakish aspect in the glow, reminding her of the young man he had once been.

The earl grimaced at the rawness of the wound. "It might indeed be wise to shave the hair off around it," he said.

Aria's eyes fluttered to Clarissa, but she said nothing.

"I'm able to apply lotion through her hair, Lord Kinsford," Clarissa assured him.

"But how will it heal with all that hair? At least right at the wound the hair could be snipped away." He turned to his sister. "Aria, it's not as though you'll have a great bald spot, for heaven's sake. The hair above will cover any little patch we must remove."

"I don't wish you to do it," she said flatly, tossing her head. "The doctor didn't say it had to be done."

Kinsford suddenly backed off. With a smile he

said, "Very well. I'm sure he knows best. Perhaps Miss Driscoll would leave the candle so we can go over your watercolors. I'd like you to tell me about them."

Clarissa was amused to be so handsomely dismissed. She placed the candle on a table and handed him the sketch book which lay hidden under the open copy of *Evelina*. As Clarissa slipped out of the room, she heard the earl make a handsome remark about the uniqueness of subject and spirit in Lady Aria's work.

Ready for the pot of tea Meg would have prepared, Clarissa moved to the dining parlor. For a while she could hear a low murmur of voices from the sitting room. As she drank her tea she worked out on a sheet of foolscap just where she would plant the herbs in the kitchen garden next week. The weather was getting finer by the day and the chances of a late frost were low. If the lemon thyme were kept close to the cottage, if would do better; the sweet marjoram and basil could stand more exposure. When the earl spoke behind her, Clarissa started, so deep was she in her plans.

"Excuse me," he said stiffly. "I thought you must have heard me come out of the sitting room."

She pushed aside the sheet of foolscap. "No, but it is of no importance. Is Lady Aria in need of something?"

"She's fallen asleep."

He didn't seem to know quite how to proceed and Clarissa waved him to a seat at the table. When he hesitated, she said, "Please. We should discuss matters. I fear you're vexed with me."

He did not deny it. Meg had set two cups on the table and Clarissa lifted the pot with a query in her eyes. He nodded. "No milk, thank you. We got used to tea without milk on the Peninsula and I continue to drink it that way."

After she had poured his tea, she offered him the plate of biscuits that she herself had ignored. Meg had obviously put them out for the sole purpose of tempting Lord Kinsford, and she succeeded. He helped himself to one of the soft molasses treats, tasted it and his brows lifted. "If your maid serves these to the children, it's no wonder they so much enjoy coming here."

"That must be the secret," Clarissa said, her eyes dancing. "There couldn't be any other excuse for their enjoying their time in my home."

"I didn't mean to insult you, Miss Driscoll. Merely to praise the biscuits."

"I know what you meant." She forced herself to meet those intense blue eyes. "For a man of your experience, you are sometimes less than successful in dealing with the young members of your family. Both William and Lady Aria seem to expect nothing from you but scolds and discipline. I realize you are unaccustomed to handling such spirited young people, but somehow I think you might manage it better."

"This is plain speaking," he rejoined. "I had no idea we were on such terms as to admit of your dressing me down, Miss Driscoll."

His set-down was lost on her. "My concern is not with protocol, nor with preserving your more tender sensibilities, sir, but with the integrity and happiness of my pupils. I am not even concerned with your allowing them to remain my pupils," she said, forestalling him. "I have already achieved a great fondness for them, and am perfectly prepared to champion their cause whether or not it drives you to remove them from my tutelage. Though, to be honest, I should very much dislike running a dame school."

Startled, he asked, "A dame school? What has that to say to anything?"

"Nothing, I dare say. It was merely an aside, Lord Kinsford. Just now you dealt with Aria fairly well, so perhaps you could clarify something for me. Is it ordinarily your *intention* to upset her, or do you merely feel it is your *duty*?"

"Miss Driscoll, I do not have to answer to you for my behavior toward my siblings. Your own behavior, it seems to me, is not above reproach." He regarded her closely, leaning slightly forward in his chair.

Clarissa refused to honor this remark with an acknowledgment or a defense. She regarded him with mild interest, and said nothing. There was a long, pregnant silence between them before he finally said, "I am, of course, referring to your entertaining a gentleman without proper chaperonage."

Still Clarissa said nothing. Her cheeks did not color up, and her hands did not twitch with agitation. She sipped from the teacup and awaited further developments.

"My younger brother noted that he himself had provided chaperonage this morning."

Clarissa's eyes sparkled and a trill of laughter escaped her. "I did wonder why he hung about us and talked so astonishingly of going into a profession."

Kinsford was surprised into saying, "Going into a profession? Will?"

"Yes, that's what I thought. The military, he decided, as none of the others were particularly eligible. Mr. Traling did mention that they might not be in need of officers at just this moment.''

The mention of Mr. Traling's name brought Kinsford back to his grievance. ''It is no good saying you have chaperonage from your companion, since by all accounts she is rarely with you. I can't think what you're about, entertaining a man in your home under those circumstances.''

''Oh, yes, you can.'' Clarissa made a wide gesture with her hands. ''You can well imagine the unseemly things that occur when Mr. Traling comes to see me at ten o'clock in the morning.''

''The hour has very little to do with it,'' Kinsford insisted. ''That sort of thing can go on at any time of day.''

''By 'that sort of thing,' are we referring to an illicit liaison, Lord Kinsford?'' Clarissa asked, grinning at him.

He seemed suddenly to realize the ludicrousness of such a suggestion. Gruffly, because he was not at all satisfied with the direction of the conversation, he said, ''I'm not suggesting there is anything of that nature happening here, Miss Driscoll. It's the appearance of impropriety which must be attended to. You know what a small village is.''

''Yes, I do, and that is why I have Lorelia Snolgrass. If she's very seldom here, I can hardly curtail my cousin's visits until she returns, can I?''

''Your cousin? Mr. Traling is your cousin?''

''Of a sort. He is not a first cousin, if that is all that will satisfy you.''

''Where does he live, Mr. Traling? How often does he come here?''

''You cannot seriously expect me to satisfy your curiosity on such matters, Lord Kinsford. Perhaps one day you will encounter Mr. Traling, and you can discuss them with him. He's a very open, straight-forward young man. I dare say he would be pleased to fill you in on all the relevant information.''

"It's not a matter of idle curiosity, Miss Dris-coll." The earl took another bite of the molasses biscuit before continuing with great earnestness. "My sister's upbringing is of major concern to me. It would not do at all to have her stigmatized by her attendance in your house."

"I'm not aware of any stigma attached to visiting me. In fact, you seem to be the only person in the whole county who has ever thought to question my virtue." Clarissa managed a plaintive sigh. "I sup-pose right now they are saying, 'Well, what is he doing at her house this hour of the night? The sister is sick, no effective chaperone there. *That sort of thing* could be going on at this very moment.' But you would not wish me to send you away, for fear of such talk, would you?"

"No one is saying any such thing," he retorted. "They know I'm here to visit my sister, and that she is very ill. It's only natural that I would come to see her."

"Perhaps. But your mother didn't come with you. Nor did your brother. And there are only a sick girl and a maid in the house to give the appearance of propriety. All I'm saying is that it is a matter of perspective. Frankly, I can't think that anyone is in-terested enough in my affairs to concern themselves with what is going on in my cottage."

He snorted. "You aren't naive enough to believe that."

"You haven't the slightest idea how naive I am, sir."

He regarded her speculatively for a moment. Clarissa saw him take in her cap, her face (no longer in the first bloom of youth), and her figure hidden under an India shawl. And she imagined he would remember that she had not even had on shoes when he visited her the previous morning. Eccentric, yes, but doubtless not the village loose woman. He tapped impatient fingers on the shining table. Before he could speak, there was a knock at the door and soon Meg was ushering William into the small dining parlor.

"Evening, Miss Driscoll. I thought I might find you here, Kinsford. Good biscuits, aren't they? Meg is a gem." He took a third chair with very little prompting and helped himself to the molasses treats. "Meant to be by earlier but a friend from school stopped on his way through. How's Aria?"

They explained the situation and Will pursed his lips. "She's going to be all right, isn't she?"

"I think so," Clarissa assured him. "She's sleeping now."

The earl rose abruptly and said, "We should leave Miss Driscoll in peace, William. Having Aria is taking up a great deal of her time."

Obediently, his brother rose, but before he left the house, William managed to whisper to Clarissa, "I have something special for you. I'll bring it by first thing in the morning."

Oh, wonderful, Clarissa thought as she gathered the shawl more closely about her and went in search of her book. Heaven knew what William would consider an auspicious gift under the circumstances. Clarissa could scarcely contain her curiosity.

8

Clarissa slept restlessly. Her small bedchamber, one of two at the front of the house on the first floor, felt airless and cramped. Climbing out of bed, she slipped her feet into comfortable, worn slippers and drew a woolen wrap about herself. At the window overlooking the street she could see no light in the whole town. Doubtless it was the middle of a moonless night.

Off to the right lay the fields of one of the more prosperous farms in the neighborhood. To the left lay several houses on the main street which crossed her lane. Nothing stirred. Obviously it was not a sound from without that had wakened her. And the house itself was quiet. Even the small fire in the grate was totally out now. But it wasn't cold, either, that had awakened her, for the room was not particularly chill.

Still, she could not contemplate returning to her bed. Something tugged at her, refusing her peace. Aria had been resting quietly when she came upstairs, but that was no guarantee that she remained well. Clarissa hastily lit a candle and moved silently through the hall and down the stairs to the ground floor. The sitting-room door was closed, to keep the warmth of the fire within the room as long as possible.

She opened the door noiselessly, not wanting to awaken her patient. Her eyes went directly to the sofa and found it empty. Clarissa's heart lurched in her chest. The candle shook slightly in her hand. It was not a large room, though the largest in the cottage. Even given the inky shadows of the corners of the room, Clarissa could tell at a glance that Lady Aria was not there.

Back in the hall Clarissa checked to see that the front door was closed and bolted, as was their habit at night. Lady Aria could not have gone out that way. The dining parlor across the hall was as empty as the sitting room, though Meg had set dishes out for Clarissa's breakfast.

The kitchen, just beyond the dining parlor, had a door to the outside, and Clarissa hastened to check whether it was locked like the front door. But in the kitchen itself, standing at the larder in her bare feet, was Lady Aria. Clarissa wasn't sure that the girl was fully awake, and she had heard it was unwise to abruptly awaken a person who was walking in her sleep. So she whispered Lady Aria's name from the doorway and the girl immediately looked up. She had no candle and the room, save for the flickering gleam of Clarissa's, was in darkness.

"They don't feed us enough at school," Lady Aria said distinctly and defiantly. "I'm quite hungry, and it's because the stew this evening was very skimpy on the meat. I'm getting myself a little something to eat."

Lady Aria hadn't been at school for the last year, owing to her extreme dislike of the place. Clarissa decided to go along with the girl rather than attempt to disabuse her of her notion of where she was. "I'm quite famished myself," she said. "Let's see what we can find, shall we?"

There was a bit of cold mutton, some baked plum pudding and a bit of stewed rhubarb which Clarissa heaped onto a serving platter and carried to the dining parlor. Lady Aria followed her obediently and sat down, prepared to be served whatever was available. Clarissa took utensils and plates from the sideboard and dished up as much as she felt Lady Aria could possibly handle after having had so little for the past two days. There were several candles on the table and she lit them, illuminating a very strange scene indeed.

This was certainly disorientation, and yet, as before, it seemed to come from the situation. This time Aria's empty stomach had recalled other such occasions and confused the two. She was now eating with simple pleasure and looked across at Clarissa with a dawning comprehension. "What time is it, Miss Driscoll?" she asked, a trifle hesitantly.

"I don't know precisely. I haven't actually seen a clock, but I suspect it's the middle of the night."

"Yes, that's what I thought." Lady Aria shifted uncomfortably in her chair. "Do you often eat in the middle of the night?"

"No, my dear, but you were particularly hungry and so we're having a bit of a meal to see us through the night." Clarissa cocked her head at the girl. "Do you remember why you're here?"

"I had an accident." Lady Aria frowned. "I get a little confused sometimes. Things don't quite fit together." Her face crumpled and a tear drifted down her cheek. "There's something wrong with my head, isn't there?"

"I doubt very much if it's anything permanent, Lady Aria," Clarissa reassured her, reaching across the small table to squeeze the young woman's hand. "You've had a bad blow to the head, and a fever. It's going to take a while for your body to accommodate all that. Try not to worry yourself about it. Dr. Lawrence is keeping an eye on you, and he's very capable."

‹ The tears in Aria's eyes shone in the candlelight. "But what if it doesn't go away? What if I'm always . . . wrong in the head?"

Clarissa wanted to dismiss the thought, but felt that Aria deserved a proper answer. "I can't think of anyone whose family would more easily accept such a situation. They love you and have the means to sustain you in whatever condition you should find yourself. But, my dear, it simply isn't going to be a problem, I feel certain. Look how your appetite has improved!"

Though this spoke to nothing in particular, Lady Aria seemed cheered. "Yes," she agreed, "I do seem to have a remarkable appetite. I must be improving." The moisture in her eyes gradually diminished as she helped herself to the plum pudding and the stewed rhubarb. "I'm so glad there weren't any vegetables," she said, an impish grin lighting her face.

Clarissa felt as reassured by the grin as she had been shaken by the earlier events. It might, however, be wise to mention these mental aberrations to the doctor, since he hadn't been witness to any of them. They could be nothing, or they could be very important. She would have to tell the earl, too, to keep him fully apprised of the situation.

When Lady Aria had finished her impromptu meal,

she unconsciously rubbed her injured shoulder. "It's time you were back in bed," Clarissa insisted, standing up and coming around to the girl's side. "If you think a bed upstairs would be more commodious than the sofa, we could take you up there."

Aria covered a yawn with her hand. "No, thank you. I'll be asleep in no time on the sofa." She winced as she rose from the chair but managed to walk, rather gingerly, back to the sitting room. Without any further discussion, she climbed onto the sofa, pulled the covers up about her shoulders, and proceeded to fall asleep.

Clarissa tucked the covers under her and watched the deep, even breathing of her patient. The girl's forehead was no warmer than earlier in the evening, so there was no recurrence of high fever. Clarissa returned to the dining parlor to return the remaining food to the larder. Then, almost reluctantly, she retired upstairs to her bed.

William rose early the next morning. He had determined that it would be best to take care of an urgent matter before his brother discovered what was going on. Though Will had been annoyed with Upton for bringing the dog to him, he had felt he must indeed take charge of the little terrier, since it had been he who had first suggested the plan of heisting the small beast. Not that they had intended keeping it, and in fact it had been returned to its master once already.

"Only it was the shabbiest thing," Upton had protested as he tied the dog by a strong rope in the stables of Kinsford Hall. "The master said he had no intention of teaching the little brute any manners, and within four-and-twenty hours the terrier had bitten two more boys. It's the flapping gowns," Upton declared. "I swear if a bishop were to rush by him with his robes flapping, the dog would take a chunk out of his leg."

"But what am I to do with him?" Will asked. "Can't very well have him biting everybody about the place."

"That's what I'm *telling* you," Upton insisted. "He don't just bite everybody. Only the ones in flapping robes who are rushing by. Promise you it's the truth. We had ever such an easy ride here with him on my lap. Kept licking me. Disgusting."

"Kinsford isn't half fond of terriers," Will mused. "I suppose I could leave him in the barn, but that would be taking a chance of his nipping at the horses. Dashed inconvenient!"

Upton disregarded this problem. "He isn't likely to attack the horses. Then again, who knows. I'd keep him in the house if it were me. Perhaps your mother would like a lap dog."

The two young men regarded the terrier happily scratching at his shoulder. Though small and golden, the dog did not look quite like a comfortable house pet. He was scruffy and tended to be excitable, even when not inclined to bite anyone. It was his barking that brought the head groom out to investigate.

"What have we here?" asked Perkins. "Can't have an animal in the stables, Master William. It's likely to upset the horses."

"It's only overnight," Will had assured him. "No need to mention it to Kinsford."

And there the matter had rested. But Will had hit on a brilliant solution the previous evening and he was up betimes to carry it out: for Perkins was not one to keep mum any longer than the promised period of time, and Will wanted the dog gone before Kinsford put in his morning appearance at the stables. In his own mind, Will had justified the kidnaping by believing quite firmly that anyone who didn't care properly for a dog (which included, in his opinion, making sure that the dog didn't injure anyone) did not deserve to have one.

True, Will had not been able to gain Miss Driscoll's permission on the previous evening because his brother had been with her, but he felt certain she would be delighted to have the animal. Why, she hadn't even a cat! And it was no use saying that the dog would cost her anything, for he himself would see that she was supplied with scraps from the Hall. Obviously it was the most perfect of schemes, and he had no hesitation in taking the dog along with him. After all, wouldn't the little beast simply steal her heart?

Perkins handed up the dog once Will was astride Rannoch, who was not at all happy about the arrangement. The little dog, who had ridden quite easily with Upton the previous day (by report), now managed to scrabble about on Will's lap and scrape his paws along the horse's back. It was all Will could do to control the two of them, and he rather wished he'd brought a sack for the dog. The little animal whined and barked and generally raised quite a ruckus for such a small thing. Will wouldn't have owned him for the world.

But he was sure Miss Driscoll would love him.

"No," she said. "I don't want a dog."

"But, Miss Driscoll, he's perfect. Such a small, cute thing. And so friendly." He was licking Miss Driscoll's ankles at the time. "You'll have grown so used to Aria's company that you'll be lonely when she leaves. You'll need a dog to keep you company."

"Thank you, William. I'm sure it's very considerate of you, but I determined some little while ago that I would not have a pet, and I see no reason to break that rule."

"But why? There's nothing like the company a dog gives." This determined instruction was offered over a chorus of barks by the dog, who was running round and round Miss Driscoll's hall.

"Yes, I see," she said, dampingly. "What's his name?"

Will considered this a good sign, her asking the dog's name; unfortunately he did not remember it, if he had ever known it. "Terry," he said, almost adding, "for terrier."

"And where did he come from?"

"A master at school, who was unable to care for him properly." That suggested a new line of persuasion to Will. "He really hasn't had the kind of care you could give him, Miss Driscoll. He needs some affection, don't you know? And you mustn't think he would be a burden. He hardly eats anything, and I'll have the kitchens at the Hall send down scraps for him. Damme, I'll bring them myself!"

Clarissa crossed her arms over her chest. It was a stance Will knew as unpromising in his brother, and he hastened to pick up the animal and hold him out to her. "Here. Just see what a sweet little fellow he is."

Reluctantly, Clarissa accepted the small burden. The dog did not particularly like being held, but he looked up at her with curious brown eyes and she sighed. "Well . . ."

From the sitting room they heard Aria's voice calling, "Is there a dog here? Have you my brought my Puffin?"

Perfect, Will thought. Now Aria would be on his side, too. He slipped into the sitting room before Miss Driscoll could prevent him. She was forced to follow with the dog in her arms. "No, I haven't brought Puffin," Will explained, "but I've brought a dog for Miss Driscoll, and he'll keep you company while you're here, too." Inspiration hit again and he turned to Clarissa to say, "And what a grand companion he'll make on your walks, ma'am. He has lots of energy."

Clarissa could undoubtedly see that for herself. The animal wanted down and she set him on the floor. He instantly bounded up onto the sofa with Lady Aria and proceeded to lick her face. She giggled and wrapped her arms around him. "What's his name?"

"Terry."

"Ugh. I think we should change it," she decreed. "I bet he won't mind. How about Max, for Maximilian?"

"Well, he's Miss Driscoll's dog, so she should be the one to decide," Will said, transparent with the effort to unburden himself of the animal.

Clarissa shook her head helplessly. "I'm not at all certain I want to keep the dog, William. Though perhaps we could have him while Lady Aria is here. He seems to have taken an instant fancy to her."

And indeed he did. The terrier had already curled up beside the girl, and fallen asleep. Will decided it would be pointless to press the matter, and he felt certain that Miss Driscoll would be unable to part with the dog once she had spent a little time with him, provided the animal didn't bark its fool head off.

"So we shall call him Max, shall we?" Lady Aria asked, laying a hand possessively on the dog's head.

Clarissa and William agreed. Will inquired after his sister's health, but he was rather in a hurry to be off, so that no one would change their minds. And so that his brother would not find him there, in possession of the dog. For some unknown reason it did not occur to Will that his older brother might ask Miss Driscoll, or even his sister, the origins of the newest member of the Driscoll household. In Will's mind, once a pet was established in a house, he was simply a part of the fixtures. One might ask an animal's name, or of what breed it was, but was one really likely to ask whence it had come? William thought not. And William was wrong.

"Where did the dog come from?" Lord Kinsford asked in astonishment when he found it lying on Aria's bed, snuggled up against her.

"Will brought him this morning. Isn't he the dearest thing?" Aria asked.

Kinsford frowned. "Where did Will get him? He's certainly not from the Hall. We've never had a cairn terrier there that I can recall."

Miss Driscoll was not present at this interview, and Aria had not learned Max's previous abode, so she simply dismissed the question. "He likes me," she said. "He took to me instantly. Jumped right up on the sofa with me when Miss Driscoll put him on the floor."

"I don't suppose he's the animal who startled your horse," Kinsford muttered, more or less to himself. "That one was much larger. But what was Will doing with a dog?" Something resonated in his mind, but he was unable to quite place what nagged at him about the animal.

"I'm feeling much better today," Aria interjected, a little annoyed with him for concentrating on the dog and not on her own condition. It also seemed possible to her that Will might have some reason not to disclose the animal's past, for where indeed would he have gotten it?

Kinsford was instantly distracted. "I'm glad to hear it. You had a restful night, then?"

This easy question seemed to discompose her a little. Aria decided it would be best for Miss Driscoll to broach the night's adventure with the earl and so she said, "Well, I did wake hungry in the middle of the night and had something to eat. Then I fell instantly back to sleep."

Told in such a way, it sounded tame enough. Aria and Will were in the habit of telling Kinsford the truth, but seldom the whole truth. He did make such a fuss about one's obligations and duties! Lady Aria didn't want to make him suspicious.

Kinsford stayed to visit with her for some time. He had brought a pack of cards for her and showed her a game of solitaire that she had not known before. So she was well pleased with him by the time he took his leave. The dog wasn't mentioned again.

9

Since Miss Driscoll had left them alone, he felt he should make his good-byes to her in person. The house was so tiny he felt she could be nowhere but in the dining parlor, and he tapped on the open door. Miss Driscoll bid him enter and he found her there with an account book which she closed on his entering.

"Aria seems well this morning," he said. "In case I should miss him, I wish you would ask Dr. Lawrence if it is safe to bring her home now."

"Please sit down, Lord Kinsford," she said, looking a little troubled.

He was not in the mood to have an argument with her, and he hesitated. "I don't want to keep you from your business, Miss Driscoll. Perhaps I should be on my way."

"There have been two occasions on which Lady Aria has exhibited distinct disorientation," she said, halting his attempted leave-taking. "I think we should discuss them."

Kinsford drew up a chair and seated himself. "I beg your pardon. She seemed so well this morning."

"And I believe she is." Clarissa's hands moved restlessly in her lap. "But we shouldn't overlook these instances just because she comes out of them quickly and seems so much healed.''

''Tell me what happened.''

''The first time,'' Clarissa said, her brows drawn down with concentration, ''she awoke from sleep and asked for her watercolors, as though she were here for a lesson. She wanted to paint the ha-ha and William chasing a fox cub, but she spoke of it as if it had just happened. When I reminded her that she was ill, she recollected herself immediately. It was as brief as that, and I was willing to believe it was just the influence of a dream, and the normal confusion of being sick and away from her own room. Perhaps I should have said something.''

The earl was inclined to dismiss the occurrence and assured her that she had not been at fault in allowing it to pass. It could have happened to anyone, awakening from a dream. ''What was the second occasion?'' he asked.

''I woke in the middle of the night last night, not aware of any sound having disturbed my sleep. Lady Aria had seemed well enough and neither I nor Meg had thought it necessary to sit with her. Still, I felt it wise to check on her, since I was awake. It gave me quite a start to find her missing from the sitting room.''

''Gone from the sofa? Where was she?''

''In the kitchen, looking for some food. We've been feeding her a very light diet and she sometimes fell asleep before eating all of that, so I'm not surprised that she was hungry. But she didn't know where she was. She thought she was in the kitchen at school, foraging some food. She remained under that impression, even though we talked for several minutes, only coming to understand where she was when we had been seated at the dining table and eating for a while.''

Kinsford felt a frisson of fear. He said nothing, but waited to hear the conclusion of Miss Driscoll's tale.

''After a while she asked me what time it was, and seemed to understand who and where she was. But it frightened her. She said she got a little confused and that things didn't quite fit together sometimes. She wondered if there was something wrong with her head.''

''Oh, God. The poor child. She mentioned nothing of this to me this morning.''

''No, I suspected not. And it may be nothing, but I doubt her fear has entirely gone away. I will, of course, mention it to Dr. Lawrence this time and hear what he has to say. You might wish to consult him yourself.''

''Yes. I'll stay in the village until he comes. No, no, not here, thank you. We have imposed quite enough on you.'' He impulsively covered her hand, which lay on the arm of her chair, with his. ''You've been extraordinarily kind, Miss Driscoll. Forgive my foul temper these last few days. I have no excuse for it. I've meant to do right by the children but it's making up a bit late, I fear. My stepmama seems a great deal less able to manage than I had realized.'' He rose quickly to his feet and added, ''We'll talk again after the doctor has been here.''

He was gone before Clarissa could reply. She stared unseeing for some time at her hand, warmed so unaccountably by his touch, before she retrieved the accounts book.

Clarissa soon heard the clicking of the dog's nails on the floor in the hall. It seemed to her that the little fellow might need to go outside, so she went out to find him sitting in front of the front door, staring at it as if it would open of its own accord. Since Clarissa was not at all worried that Max would wander off (in fact, rather hoped that he would), she allowed him to go out on his own.

She found Aria sound asleep, looking almost angelic on the sofa. The playing cards had fallen onto the floor and Clarissa bent to retrieve them. There was a sack there of other items Lord Kinsford had brought his sister, including some ribbons for her hair, another note from her mama, a book of Cowper's verses, and a nightdress of her own. She'd been wearing Clarissa's, which were a little long for her, and which somehow made Clarissa feel uncomfortable when Lord Kinsford was about, as though her nightdress should have been somehow different—prettier, or softer, or warmer, or something.

The dog scratched vigorously at the front door and Clarissa hastened to spare the wooden surface. Max trotted in as if he'd owned the place for his entire life. His exploration of the cottage then began, first heading back down the hall to the kitchen. Clarissa followed him and found him perched on his haunches, begging food from the astonished Meg.

"Where did he come from, Miss Clarissa?" Meg asked. "I've not seen him around the village."

"He's ours," her mistress informed her ruefully, "if we'll keep him. William brought him by this morning. Aria has renamed him Max."

"Cute little fellow," Meg allowed as she cut off a bite of the boiled beef and offered it to the dog. "Were you wanting a dog?"

"No, and I'm not at all sure I shall allow him to

remain. But he seems to delight Aria, and curled right up with her. I can only think he'll do her good for the time being.''

"Yes, miss." Meg dug through a cabinet to find a battered bowl which she filled with water and placed on the floor near the back door. "We always had a dog when I was growing up. They're not much bother."

Clarissa shook her head, but not in disagreement. "We'll see."

The dog, through with his exploration of the kitchen, retraced his path to the dining parlor, which he trotted around with nose to floor. Finding no crumbs of interest, he traveled out to the hall and up the narrow staircase to the floor above. Clarissa followed him. There were three rooms on the first floor: her bedroom, that of her "companion," and a room at the back which was Meg's bed-sitting room. Finding the door to this last closed, he barked at it, but Clarissa hushed him and said, "You can't go in there, Max. Not unless you're invited. Come and see mine."

He obediently followed her into the larger of the front rooms, where he instantly bounded onto the bed. Clarissa felt she should decide just as instantly whether he was to be allowed such a liberty. Easier to give in later than to change an established habit, she decided, and she ordered him off the bed. Max looked definitely put out by her insistence, but he crawled under the bed, lay down, and remained there.

The sound of a carriage stopping in the lane outside her house drew her to the window. Dr. Lawrence was arriving in the gig he drove on occasion. He tied the reins to an iron ring beside her door and pulled down his medical bag from the seat. Before he had even lifted the brass knocker on the door, Lord Kinsford was striding down the lane toward him and he waited until the earl was abreast of him before rapping.

Looking down unobserved, Clarissa realized what a striking figure Alexander Barrington made. He was no more than average height, but there was something so powerful, so commanding about his presence that one would not have passed him even on the streets of London without a second glance. She had thought, at one time, that it was simply his consciousness of his rank.

Now she was not at all sure this was true. Certainly he never forgot that he was an earl, but there was something more. An intensity, a vigorous strength to him that she was unfamiliar with in other men, and which was a little disconcerting. With difficulty had she maintained her poise on the occasions he had seemed intent on having his way. The force of his will was immense, but it was only part of the influence she felt.

Abruptly Clarissa turned away from the window. She had seen the two men enter the house and knew she would be called upon to recite her story to Dr. Lawrence. The dog remained under the bed when she left the room and proceeded down the stairs to the hall where she found Meg taking the two men's hats and coats. She nodded to Lord Kinsford and smiled at the doctor. "We can talk more easily in the dining parlor," she suggested, and the two men followed her there.

When Dr. Lawrence had heard of the two episodes with Lady Aria, he looked concerned. "It's not something to be wished for," he said. "The disorientation may mean pressure in her head which is affecting her mental processes and could lead to problems. I don't mean to be an alarmist, however. I've seen patients with far greater disorientation settle down to perfect recovery."

"Is there anything we can do about it?" Lord Kinsford asked.

"Just continue the compresses and the fever medication for the time being. Tomorrow, if she's had any more disorientation, I'll bleed her a little. But she's a healthy young thing and I think we must surely hope for the best. Let me have a look at her now."

In the sitting room Lady Aria blinked awake at the touch of Dr. Lawrence's hand on her forehead. She looked momentarily puzzled, then understanding. "I'm a little better today," she announced rather weakly. "Perhaps not up to the jolting of a carriage ride home, though."

Dr. Lawrence was looking at the wound on her head and into her eyes. "No," he agreed, giving the matter some thought, "I think what would be best is if we simply got you out of Miss Driscoll's sitting room and up to the spare room above. I know you'd like to be in your own bed, my dear, but this is the safer alternative."

He looked at the earl, who shrugged helplessly. "We'll do whatever is best for my sister, of course," Kinsford said. "I do hate to impose on Miss Driscoll for any longer than necessary."

"I'm delighted to be of assistance," Clarissa assured him.

"But what of your companion? Won't Aria be displacing her?"

"Lorelia is not expected back for some time."

Clarissa said this with laughing eyes, but the earl did not seem to notice. "I'll have Meg prepare the room."

When suitable arrangements had been made, Kinsford asked his sister, "Shall I carry you upstairs?"

"Oh, no. I can surely walk that distance." Aria accepted Clarissa's hand to help her off the sofa. But it was obvious from her tentative footsteps that she was feeling fragile. Kinsford offered his arm in the most gallant way, but at the narrow stairs there was no possibility of their walking side by side. Aria cast her eyes upward with a rather worried look; she hadn't been much on her feet for several days and the stairs were a little steep. Kinsford offered again to carry her.

"That might be wise," Clarissa interjected, fearing her guest's pride might stand in her way. "So long as he doesn't bang your head against the wall."

Aria giggled and agreed. Kinsford lifted her with gentle ease. Clarissa led the way, and pushed open the door of a charming room under the eaves. Meg had turned down the bed and put a warming pan in to make it toasty. Kinsford set his sister down and watched as she climbed into the high half-tester bed. There was a colorful coverlet with matching draperies at the windows. A rocking chair sat on a Turkey carpet, with a lamp and a shelf of books to hand. On the dressing table were various items of feminine toilette and a letter. Clarissa flashed Meg, who was removing the warming pan, an appreciative glance.

The earl looked around the small room while trying to appear nonchalant and uninterested. His sister spoke the words that he was obviously thinking.

"So this is Miss Snolgrass's room," Aria declared, her eyes wide with curiosity. "How very cozy. I wonder that with such a room she finds it bearable to be away so frequently."

"I'm so glad you like it. Lorelia would be pleased." Clarissa plumped up the pillow and added, "You are to make yourself perfectly at home. Use the drawers and the wardrobe, and see if there is any reading matter that appeals to you. I'm sure Max will be happy to keep you company."

At Kinsford's startled look, Clarissa reminded him, "The dog. Max is currently curled up under my bed, but he'll be delighted to find an occupant here. He's a friendly soul."

"Oh, yes," Aria agreed. "Would you get him for me, Alexander?"

The earl, who was not in the habit of wandering around people's homes uninvited, especially not those of young women in the country, protested. Clarissa was in the midst of measuring some of the fever mixture for her patient and she assured Kinsford that it would be perfectly all right for him to step next door and entice Max from his new resting spot.

Before he returned, the dog came charging through the door, emitting piercing yaps of excitement. Dr. Lawrence frowned at the ruckus. "Lady Aria should have complete quiet in which to rest," he said, regarding the dog doubtfully.

Max bounded onto the bed and thrust his little muzzle under Aria's hand. She laughed and said, "He'll be quiet for me, Dr. Lawrence. And if he's not, I shan't mind."

Belatedly Kinsford made an appearance, complaining, "I thought he was going to take a chunk out of my ankle. It's a good thing I had boots on.

Aria, I'm not at all sure he's a fit companion for a sick girl."

Aria's face grew stormy. Clarissa made no attempt to intervene. She was not convinced that she wanted a pet, even for the duration of Aria's stay. She could abide by Kinsford's decision on Max, whichever way it went. The brother and sister regarded each other with a heightening tension. It was Dr. Lawrence who spoke first.

"These little dogs are occasionally averse to men. I've never known them to bite a woman. But mind you, Lady Aria, if his yapping keeps you awake so you don't get your proper rest, he shall have to go." He turned to Lord Kinsford, with a persuasive smile. "Would that be satisfactory, sir? She seems quite taken with the little animal."

Kinsford hesitated. His gaze momentarily rested on Clarissa, who gave no sign of her opinion one way or the other. Eventually he shrugged. "Very well. He can stay if he behaves himself. And if Miss Driscoll is willing to put up with him."

"Well, of course she is," Aria said with exasperation. "Will gave the dog to her."

"Very thoughtful of him," Kinsford murmured, as Clarissa remarked rather ambiguously, "Then it's settled. I think we should leave Lady Aria so she can get some rest."

As the doctor prepared to leave, Kinsford said, "I should like a word with Miss Driscoll before I go," and waited while Dr. Lawrence gathered up his hat and gloves from the hall stand.

Clarissa then led him into the sitting room, which had already been tidied by Meg. It was rather a relief to have the room returned to its original purpose. She motioned to a chair as she took her accustomed seat on the sofa. There was a moment of silence as he seemed to organize his thoughts. His hands, strong but still, rested on his thighs.

"Aria seems to be feeling all right at the moment, but she could easily become confused again," he said. "I would offer, and am offering, to send someone from the Hall to keep watch over her at night, if you think that would be wise. Or if you could tolerate another person in your house."

"I'm a light sleeper, Lord Kinsford. I think if she woke at night and moved about I would hear her." Clarissa frowned. "But I might not, and I would hate for her to come to any harm."

Kinsford said ruefully, "I dare say the dog would cause a commotion if Aria got up at night. That should be alarm enough."

"Yes. But if you would feel more comfortable having someone from the Hall sit with her . . ."

He seemed to consider the matter, his brows lowering over his astute blue eyes. Eventually he said, "Let's leave things as they are for the moment. If she should seem more disoriented, we might want to have someone with her. But for now . . ." He shrugged. "She's likely to sleep through the night with no problems."

There was a knock at the door. Clarissa assumed it would be William, coming to check on his sister again. But she heard Steven Traling's voice from the hallway and saw Lord Kinsford's face tighten. He rose instantly to take his leave, and his voice, which had been thoughtful and kind, now had a slight edge.

"If this all becomes too much for you to handle, Miss Driscoll, we will certainly manage to move my sister to the Hall without any damage. Good day."

As he received his hat from Meg, Clarissa saw

him nod minimally to Steven. Steven, never one to notice a slight, bowed to the earl, and said cheerfully, "How's our patient today?" It would have been difficult to know precisely what Kinsford said in reply, since he closed the door behind himself as he spoke.

10

Clarissa felt annoyed with Steven for showing up just then. This was an irrational annoyance and she refused to think about it. Instead she welcomed him into the sitting room as cordially as she was able and seated herself once more on the sofa.

"So, your patient has left at last," he remarked, making himself comfortable.

"No, Lady Aria is still here."

"She is?" He sounded disappointed. "Where?"

"She's just upstairs in the spare room. There's some concern that the blow to her head may have done more significant damage than appeared at first. Dr. Lawrence doesn't want her bounced around, so he'd like her to stay here for a while."

Steven winced. "You mean she may be sort of odd in the head from now on?"

"Probably she'll heal perfectly, but she's had a few periods of disorientation that worry the doctor. That worry all of us."

"Wouldn't she be better off at the Hall? There are so many more people there to take care of her."

"I dare say she would be. It's just difficult to get her there without some danger of exacerbating her condition."

Steven frowned. "This has become quite a burden

to you, Clarissa. I think the earl could handle it better.''

Now Clarissa felt truly impatient with him. "It's not particularly a problem for me, and how do you propose Lord Kinsford is to change the situation?''

"Well, he could move her to Mrs. Luden's house, for one thing. Someone could carry her *that* far.''

"But I'm her teacher . . . and her friend, actually. If she's going to be in the village at all, she should be here.''

"I don't see that.''

"The only reason you don't see it is because it's disrupting your visits,'' she accused.

He was immediately contrite. "I suppose you're right,'' he agreed with a slow, rueful smile. "I wanted your full attention. Jane's parents are driving me crazy. I can't say anything, or go anywhere, without their making some comment on it. And Jane is so close to her lying-in that she doesn't seem concerned with much else. I hate living in the same house with her parents! They just ruin everything.''

"You sound like a spoiled child,'' Clarissa told him, but softened. "I know it's hard for you, Steven, especially now. But you're going to have to find a solution for yourself, and not just run to me with tales of their infamy.''

He sighed and cocked his head at her. "You didn't used to mind.''

"How do you know that?'' she asked, teasing. "True, I have felt sorry for you. And I still do, Steven. But I have someone else at the moment who has an even stronger claim on my attention. Your concerns will have to take second place for a while.'' She waved aside his protests. "Yes, I know, it's a very trying time for you. It is a frightening time for Lady Aria.''

"Does she think there's something wrong?"

"She knows things aren't quite right. I really should go up and see if she needs anything.''

"Of course." He was instantly on his feet. "But if she's asleep, Clarissa, would you take a short walk with me? Please?''

His eyes, pleading as a puppy, reminded her of Max. "I suppose we could walk the dog.''

"What dog? Since when have you a dog?"

"William brought him this morning." Clarissa brushed back a wisp of hair. She was not in the mood to explain to Max. "Don't ask. I'll be back in a while.''

Upstairs she found Aria sound asleep. Meg had placed a bell on the bedside table, ready for their patient to summon them if necessary. What a treasure Meg was! Clarissa would need to reward her for all the extra effort she was sustaining during this period, though how she was to manage this at the moment she could not quite imagine. Max lay curled against the girl but he jumped down at Clarissa's quiet summons and padded down the stairs after her.

Clarissa explained to Meg where she was going, and led her small party out of the cottage and down the lane which led to the fields beyond. Max barked excitedly, causing Steven to grimace at Clarissa. "Does he do that all the time?" he asked. "It would get on my nerves.''

"I've only had him for a few hours," Clarissa protested. "I haven't the slightest idea how much he barks. But you may be sure William can have him back if he's going to be a nuisance to me and the neighbors.''

The little dog was yapping excitedly as he scurried along the lane, sniffing at everything that came in his path. He would get ahead of them, only to circle back, enthusiastically barking as he faced them once more. Clarissa clapped her hands. "Enough, Max." He responded, to some degree, by hushing for a moment, only to yap again as he charged off.

Steven grinned at her. "He's obviously going to be easy to train. Want me to try my hand at it?"

Clarissa was not at all sure she did, but she nodded. Steven, in a commanding voice, ordered the dog to come to him. Max eyed him with suspicion for a moment, then amenably trotted back to sit down in front of him, cocking his head to one side. He looked so adorable that Clarissa couldn't help laughing. Max barked in accord.

"No!" Steven snapped his fingers and the dog regarded him curiously. And barked. Steven tapped the dog's nose and repeated his "no," and Max slunk down on his haunches as though he'd been beaten. Obviously a dog of great sensitivity, Clarissa thought.

"Now don't encourage him," Steven protested. "He'll never learn that way."

"I'd be surprised if he learned in any case," she said, and continued to walk along the lane. There was a stile onto a footpath crossing the hillock to the church and she led the way over it. Max scampered after her, ignoring Steven's command to stay. Clarissa shook her head. "Don't bother with him, Steven. I doubt if he's trainable at his age and I probably won't keep him anyhow."

"What about Lady Aria? Isn't she fond of him already?"

"Well, that's how I thought I'd get rid of him,"

Clarissa admitted. She reached down absently to pet the little dog. "She'll probably want to take him back when she returns to the Hall. So I don't intend to get too devoted to him."

The footpath was narrow and a little rough. Clarissa hadn't changed into her walking shoes and she could feel the pebbles through the thin soles of her slippers. But the day was glorious, sun streaming down and the smell of new spring growth. There were birds carolling in the bushes. Max darted about, chasing wisps of straw or blades of grass. When they came abreast of an old log, Clarissa sat down and made room for Steven.

"Aren't we going to trudge for miles?" he asked as he seated himself.

"Not today." Clarissa watched Max as he scurried off and hastened back. "How's Jane feeling? She must be due for her lying-in any day now."

"Not for a week, and her doctor said it might be two. She's a little tired and rather nervous. Things upset her easily. I seem to get on her nerves."

He looked so woebegone that Clarissa patted his hand in sympathy. "She'll get over it, you know. This isn't a time to have your feelings hurt. She's the one, after all, who's facing a frightening time."

He sighed. A frown drew down his brows. For a long time he stared off toward the horizon, where a lone tree's branches were etched against the blue sky. "One of her friends died in childbed a few weeks ago," he finally said. "We don't talk about it, but it's there between us, the fear. What if she died, Clarissa? What would I do?"

"She's not going to die," Clarissa said bracingly. "She's a healthy young woman and she's taken good care of herself during these long months. What she probably needs is a good distraction and I can't think of anyone better than you at distracting someone.''

"She'd rather have her mother there," he rejoined, morose.

"Well, her mother has had a child. It must be reassuring to talk with her."

Max returned to nudge against Clarissa's leg. She ignored him and he jumped up into her lap. Shaking her head with amused acceptance, she continued to concentrate her attention on Steven.

"Her mother keeps saying how useless men are at such a time, hinting that her husband went off hunting right when she was about to have Jane."

"Perhaps he did. You could very well be here visiting me when your own wife delivers, if you're not careful."

"I know. And I'd stay there twenty-four hours a day except that her parents drive me crazy, and Jane herself shoos me out of the house, telling me not to hang about all day, that it makes her edgy. What am I to say to that?"

"I wouldn't argue with her about it," Clarissa counseled. "And I'd make sure your whereabouts are always known, so you can be reached when she needs you." At his frown, she added, "You don't have to tell her or her parents. Perhaps you trust one of the servants, or a friend they could reach."

"Perhaps. I hate to be so tied down," he grumbled.

"I dare say your wife isn't just thrilled that she can't do whatever she wishes, either. That's simply the way things are, Steven. We'd all like to be able to do whatever we please, but it just isn't possible."

He seemed to hear a special note in her voice and

regarded her quizzically. "What would *you* want to do, Clarissa? If you could do anything you wanted."

As a game, it seemed a good distraction. But Clarissa wasn't about to tell him the whole truth. "Well, if I were rich, I'd have a home here in the country, much like Pennhurst, with a stable full of horses and lots of servants to keep all the rooms sparkling. And then I'd have a house in London, too, where I'd go for the Season. I'd see all the plays and attend all the musical evenings I could fit into my schedule."

"When did you develop this love for London?"

"My father took me there when I was younger. Perhaps half a dozen times. It was always delightful. So exciting to live amidst all that bustle. Father knew a number of fascinating people, too. Poets, painters, politicians." She smiled reminiscently, stroking the little dog in her lap. "I miss that. Not that I would have wanted to live there year-round. But to visit occasionally . . ."

"Now me, I wouldn't mind in the least living there permanently," Steven said. "Especially if Jane's parents didn't."

"You'd enjoy living anywhere they didn't," she retorted.

"Not at all! I should hate living in Yorkshire, for instance. Far too far away from everything. And too rugged for a gentle soul like me."

Clarissa appreciated his poking fun at himself. Steven was hardly a gentle soul, but restored to his usual equanimity, he was easygoing and humorous. His brightness lit her sometimes somber life. If it had been difficult for her to descend to scraping by after her former privileged life, it seemed even more formidable for the Pennwick villagers to accept her as one of them. They were polite, even kind on occasion, but they did not open their hearts to her; they could not seem to offer her friendship on an equal basis.

With Steven she could feel herself again. In many ways they offered each other the solace they found lacking in their lives. Though Clarissa didn't particularly mind giving lessons to the sons and daughters of the local gentry, it was not a lucrative endeavor and she would not like it at all if she had to open a dame school, with all its demands. Steven was the only one to whom she could confide these things, and it made her treasure his company. Not for appearances, not even for the sake of retaining the earl's brother and sister as pupils, would she have given up his visits. His wife's peace of mind, however, was a different matter.

"Jane does know that you come to visit me, doesn't she?" Clarissa asked.

Steven tugged at his earlobe, considering. "Well, I've told her that I see you sometimes. You're a relative, after all. She's suggested that you come to visit us, but you wouldn't like that."

"How do you know I wouldn't?"

"Well, because everyone would be curious about you, especially her mother. A difficult woman. She'd pry into your business, and pity you because you'd come down in the world, and just generally make you feel miserable."

"What a pleasant picture you paint!"

"Oh, you could ignore her, I suppose, but that would be rude, wouldn't it? And her father is on the loose-screw side. Well, I've told you stories about him, all of them true, I swear!"

"I've often wondered how these two paragons produced your sweet Jane."

"I credit her governess," he said, in all sincerity. "Remarkable woman. Patience of a saint, sharp as a tack. I honestly think Jane is as devoted to her as she is to her mother. Maybe more so, only she would never admit it."

"Is the governess in Bath?"

"Yes, but with another family now. She and Jane have often arranged to meet on her half-days off. I think Jane misses her, now that she hardly goes out."

Clarissa lifted Max off her lap and rose, ready to head back toward the village. "Then I think you have a perfect opportunity here to do something delightful for your wife, Steven. Arrange with the governess to come to your house to see Jane. I dare say Jane would love that."

Steven grinned. "You're right, of course. Why couldn't I have thought of such a simple thing?" And he lifted her hand to his lips and kissed it with a playful intensity. "My very dear Clarissa!"

Naturally this was the moment when Max began to bark excitedly because he'd spotted Lord Kinsford astride Longbridge approaching them. Clarissa withdrew her hand a little precipitately and Steven regarded her with mild surprise.

"He thinks there's something improper about my friendship with you," she whispered as the horse and rider drew close. Max had continued to bark and she scooped him up and held his muzzle to quiet him. She could feel a totally unwarranted flush creep into her cheeks. How very inane of her! As though she had done anything amiss.

Lord Kinsford's face wore a solemn expression which said as plainly as words that he had witnessed the episode and drawn the least favorable conclusion from it. He tipped his hat at each of them, murmuring, "Miss Driscoll, Mr. Traling," before riding off without another word.

Clarissa was tempted to let the dog have his head, since Max was growling fiercely and showed every indication of wishing to charge off after horse and rider to do great damage to one or both of them. Instead, she said, "Oh, be still, you little noise-box. Where did you learn to be so ferocious?"

"Well, I think it's the outside of enough if he entertains any such ideas," Steven said, referring to Lord Kinsford rather than the dog. "What kind of character does that give you, or me for that matter? How very odd in him to imagine such goings-on. Has he forgotten what it's like in the country?"

"Yes, I think he has." Her voice was dull, discouraged.

"Clarissa, you cannot mean that he's serious? Does he imagine we do something illicit out in the fields? No, no, he's not such a gudgeon. You've misunderstood him."

It did sound ridiculous when Steven said it and she gave a small hiccough of laughter. Then she said seriously, "He's rather stuffy where his brother and sister are concerned. There was, I believe, the suggestion that he might have to take them out of my charge."

"Nonsense! He would not be so foolish. Where could he find the kind of expertise you bring to them? There's not another soul in the neighborhood who could do half so well."

His indignation on her behalf was admirable, but irrelevant. "He's only trying to protect them, Steven. How does he know what kind of woman I am?"

"He has only to look at you to tell," Steven retorted. "The earl probably has a good working knowledge of what the other kind of woman looks like."

"Do you think so?" Her eyes danced. "I should be very surprised. He's become so righteous these last few years."

"Wasn't he like that when he was younger?"

She gave one last glance in the direction of the distant rider, then turned toward the village, Max at her ankles. "No, when he was young, he was quite wild. I remember my father talking of him, and when I'd meet him in the village I'd think he was such a daring young man, somehow *dangerous*, and I would get quite a thrill out of speaking to him. As if I were risking my reputation, or some such thing. Of course," she admitted ruefully, "he hardly noticed me at all. He was always polite but dismissive. And now he's the one who behaves ever so properly, and views me as the suspect one."

"Well, he must have a mental disorder if he suspects you of anything other than being a tiny bit unconventional." He placed her hand on his arm and matched his stride to hers. "Pay no mind to him. He's in your debt now for taking care of his sister. You haven't a thing to worry about."

Clarissa didn't quite believe she had nothing to worry about, but for the time being there was very little she could do to change the situation. So she smiled and changed the subject.

11

The Earl of Kinsford was arguing with himself. It was not something he did as a rule, and it annoyed him. Half of him seemed to believe that Miss Driscoll was exactly what she appeared to be: a spinster of some seven-and-twenty years, brought down in the world from a position of decided country eminence by her father's gambling; who now with complacence taught the sons and daughters of the neighborhood quality various accomplishments that they would otherwise not have acquired until they reached London.

The other half of Kinsford, perhaps irrationally but with some small encouragement from his own observations, believed that Miss Driscoll led a double life, which was not at all in accord with her position. This part of him believed that she only maintained the appearance of a suitable teacher for his brother and sister, that she was in actuality nothing like what appearances declared she must be.

This half of him believed that she was carrying on with Steven Traling. And it infuriated him.

The earl believed wholeheartedly that the reason it infuriated him was that he had the purity and integrity of his brother and sister to protect. The earl was, on occasion, quite able to fool himself in a spectacular way. There had been the instance of the horse which he had been determined to purchase from his friend Rutherford some years ago. But he hadn't dwelt on that after the fact, and so he had not perhaps learned the lesson it offered.

Ordinarily it was without the least difficulty that his lordship reached an opinion on any manner of subject. It was uncomfortable and somewhat perplexing for him not to understand what was going on with Miss Driscoll, especially as he was, at the moment, quite dependent on her good nature and her goodwill. Aria was ensconced in her house, next door to her bedroom, as it were, and he had to accept this arrangement or possibly jeopardize his sister's future health.

Miss Driscoll's bedroom, which he had seen that morning in retrieving the dog for his sister, had given no clue as to any sinister behavior on the spinster's part. It had been a bright, charming room with several family miniatures on the flowered-paper walls. There were a great number of books resting in a wooden trunk which served as a bookcase, and almost no toiletries on the vanity. That struck him, now, as strange. No woman of his acquaintance could manage for long without these feminine essentials. There had, in fact, been just the sort of things one would expect in Miss Snolgrass's room. Very odd, indeed.

To establish the truth of the situation Kinsford was willing to have another go-round with his younger brother, except that he realized it would do little good. Will had fixed himself as Miss Driscoll's champion. Though one could undoubtedly pick up bits and pieces from a discussion with him, there would be nothing definitive. The same could be said for any discussion with his stepmother, who knew very little about Miss Driscoll and apparently had no basis for an opinion about her of either good or ill. So how was he to go about determining the truth?

The scene he had witnessed on his ride home from the village was suspicious, certainly. One didn't every day see a young woman having her hand kissed passionately by her "cousin" in the middle of a field. That was one thing he could do, Kinsford decided. He could find out who Steven Traling was, and whether he was indeed related to Miss Driscoll. That wouldn't be so very difficult to do.

Nor would it answer most of his questions. But it was worth pursuing, just for discovering the truth of Miss Driscoll's assertions. He had the most persistent feeling that Miss Driscoll played fast and loose with the truth. And if she played fast and loose with the truth, who knew what else she played fast and loose with?

But how could she be carrying on a liaison in a small village like Pennwick where gossip was necessarily rampant about any occupant doing something untoward? The idea of gossip suddenly struck Lord Kinsford as being very useful. Though he had agreed that no servant need be sent to Miss Driscoll's house to help with Lady Aria, it now seemed the most necessary and salutory course of action. He would send a servant—Lady Aria's personal servant—and subject her to the most stringent questioning on her return. He was so taken with the idea that he sent for her immediately, to attend him in his study.

The girl's name was Betty, and she was a rather small, retiring sort of girl, though she looked vaguely familiar. Obviously nervous at being in his presence, she shrank back against the door as he outlined his directives.

"Your mistress has had a fall from her horse, as you know, Betty, and is staying at Miss Driscoll's because it would be dangerous to bring her home. Miss Driscoll has only the one servant, Meg, and I think Lady Aria's being there is more work than we should impose on the household. So I propose to send you to lend a hand."

"Yes, your lordship."

She rather squeaked this reply and he thought it prudent to inquire, "You have no objection, have you?"

"Oh, no, your lordship."

"We want Lady Aria to be perfectly comfortable there. You're to take certain foodstuffs that Mrs. Stalker will have ready for you. Probably we should send a pallet as well, so you can sleep on the floor of Lady Aria's room."

"Yes, your lordship."

"Now, Betty," he said, coming to the fine point of his instructions, "it's very important that Lady Aria not be distressed by anything at this point. She's had a concussion and at times may be disoriented. If there were anything . . . unusual or distressing going on in the household, it would not be healthy for her." His listener had developed a deep frown. "Do you understand what I'm saying, Betty?"

"You want me to spy on Miss Driscoll," she said, wide-eyed and beginning to wring her hands in front of her.

"Not at all!" he insisted, stunned by her forthrightness. "That's not what I'm asking, not in the least. I only wish to make sure Lady Aria is comfortable there. If the maid, Meg, for instance, hasn't the time to see to her wishes or. . . ."

Before he could continue, the little mouse drew herself up to her five feet of height and said with astonishing dignity, "Meg is my sister, your lordship. I know for certain she's doing everything she can to make Lady Aria comfortable. If you was to suggest otherwise to anyone, I shouldn't find it possible to remain in your employ. Your lordship."

Poor Kinsford knew when he had been defeated. "I didn't meant to suggest that your sister was doing less that she could, Betty. Not at all. She is a remarkable and resourceful girl from all I've seen. I just wish to help out in the household because of all the extra demands placed on it by my sister's presence. Certainly you would be the best person to offer assistance. If you would be so good."

Now she looked offended, as though he were mocking her in asking her permission. Which in fact perhaps he was, in an effort to maintain his own dignity. The whole situation was getting out of hand. He made a helpless gesture with his hands and Betty relented, saying with kindness, "Why, of course I shall go. There's little for me to do here with my mistress there. If that's all, your lordship?"

"Yes. Yes, that's all. Thank you, Betty. Let us know if there's anything you need there, or anything Lady Aria wants."

She curtsied and disappeared. Lord Kinsford cast his eyes heavenward and sighed. Apparently putting a spy in Miss Driscoll's household hadn't been such a terrific idea after all. He would have to manage to find out the truth on his own.

* * *

Clarissa spent an equally long time trying to sort things out in her own mind. Her discomposure at Lord Kinsford's appearance had surprised and alarmed her. Since she knew perfectly well that she was doing nothing wrong, there was no reason for her to color up at such an instance. She very much feared that she was beginning to let the earl distract her from her usual equilibrium. It had taken many years for her to achieve such serenity as she possessed and she had no intention of allowing Kinsford to destroy it.

Caught up in these musings, Clarissa did not hear Meg's announcement of William. Her attention was captured only by movement at the sitting-room door where she found William observing her with patient concern. She rose from the sofa and impulsively held out her hand. "I'm sorry, William. My mind was elsewhere."

"Oh! I thought perhaps you were ill." He shook her hand firmly and released it, still observing her closely. "Aria is a burden, I know. My brother is sending Meg's sister, Betty, to help with her care. She's Aria's maid at the Hall."

"That's very kind of the earl, though I thought we had established that it wasn't necessary." Clarissa waved him to a seat and resumed her place on the sofa. It did occur to her that the earl had made this decision after seeing her with Steven; no doubt he thought Betty's presence would inhibit such carryings on. The corners of her mouth twitched when she said to William, "I'm sure Betty will be a great help. She'll be able to report on the situation to Lord Kinsford personally."

But William had lost interest in the subject and only waited for her to finish speaking before he asked, "Where's the dog? He hasn't run away, has he?"

"Oh, no. He's curled up beside Lady Aria again. I took him for a walk earlier."

"You're going to keep him, aren't you? He's such a nice dog."

Clarissa thought her guest looked a little guilty saying this, but she assumed it was because he had dumped the animal on her with very little ceremony and felt a bit ashamed of himself over the matter. "I haven't decided yet, William. But I don't think you'll have to worry in any case. Obviously your sister has become fond of him. I'm sure she'd be happy to have him with her at the Hall."

"No, no! She can't have him there!"

Clarissa's brows rose in surprise at his adamance. "Why ever not?"

"Well, because . . . because she already has a dog. Puffin, its name is. And it wouldn't like a new dog around at all. Not at all! And I'm sure my brother can't want any more dogs. We have quite enough, in addition to Puffin." He leaned toward her, color creeping into his cheeks. "Don't even mention him to Kinsford again! It will just upset him. Not to be able to take the dog and all. He'll not want to have to disappoint Aria, but I'm quite sure he wouldn't be willing to have the dog around."

"But he's hardly ever there. What possible difference could it make to him?"

This reasoning apparently struck him forcefully. "Indeed. What difference could it make? Well, still, the dog would be better off here for a while, I think. Where it's quieter and smaller and there's someone to pay attention to him. Then later, in say a month or so, perhaps we could have him at the Hall. If you weren't willing to keep him. Would that do?''

The whole matter was beginning to seem suspicious to Clarissa, and she was about to pursue it further, when William rose abruptly. "I think I'll just look in on Aria and see if she's awake. Have a word with her, don't you know. You don't need to come up, of course. I'll just find my own way."

Clarissa shook her head ruefully. There would be plenty of time to find out what William was up to. "In a month or so" was obviously his guess as to when Kinsford would be gone again. Clarissa sighed and rose to plan menus with Meg.

William peeked around the open door of Aria's room and found her sitting up in bed with a watercolor pad on her lap and supplies at her elbow. "Well, aren't you a picture?" he teased, coming into the room. "You certainly don't look sick."

She put her finger to her lips, a wicked light sparkling in her eyes. "You're not to say that to anyone, Will," she whispered, putting aside the pad. "Close the door and I'll explain to you."

Curious, he did as he was bid, returning to the rocking chair which he overpowered with his youthful energy. "What are you up to now?" he demanded.

"Well, to be sure I'm not really well yet. My head still pounds a great deal and my shoulder and wrist ache." She shrugged such concerns aside. "But I'm not ready to go home yet, either. You must have noticed that Miss Driscoll and Kinsford do not see precisely eye to eye on things and I have decided that the longer I stay here, the more opportunity I shall have to get them to appreciate one another."

"Sounds a rather harebrained scheme to me. Just as likely they'll get on each other's nerves."

Aria tossed her head. "Little you know. Kinsford has threatened to stop my lessons with Miss Driscoll and I simply could not bear that. Now don't spoil my plan, Will, or I shall do something drastic to you when I'm better."

"I don't see how you can make them think you're sick much longer, Aria," he said reasonably. "Your color is good, and you're eating again." This much was obvious from the empty plates on her tray. He indicated the watercolor pad. "And you're even drawing again. Who would believe that you cannot be moved?"

"If I tell you, do you promise on your honor not to reveal my secret?"

Intrigued, Will nodded.

At night the village of Pennwick was almost totally silent. Its narrow lanes drifted past dark cottages, and not man or beast stirred. There were, in all, perhaps two dozen cottages in the village or close by and, for the most part, the men of the village arose early to work on one of the estates or farms, the women to join them or toil with household work and the care of children at home.

In the moonlight the houses of gray stone and red brick alike looked washed-out and insubstantial. The slate roofs and tall chimneys seemed suspended on little more than foolscap. Much more solid was the avenue of noble wych-elms on the road out of town heading toward Bath. At the other end of Pennwick was a stream thirty feet wide which was spanned by a triple-arched bridge.

Most of the cottages on the northern side of the village were joined one to the next, spare though charming, with ivy softening the roughness of the stone and sufficient windows to bring in the sunshine or moonlight. Clarissa's house, on the southern side of Pennwick, stood apart from the other cottages in the lane, and was the last one before the fields of the local farms. Out front was her small garden with hyacinths and narcissi just poking through the ground. The tulips would be protected by a small box hedge, and the scilla would grow close to the ground, its delicate blue flowers the treasure of her spring garden.

Clarissa slept soundly as usual, secure in the knowledge that Lady Aria had had a good day and that the maid Betty was established in her room to watch over her in the night. The sighing of the wind and the distant creak of the elms were the only sounds disturbing the peaceful quiet.

So it was with heart pounding that Clarissa was awakened by a cacophony of alarming proportions. There were shrieks and groans, and an incessant sharp barking that sent shivers down her spine. She bounded out of bed, pulling on the dressing gown she had left on a chair at the foot of her bed. When she burst into the hall, flinging the door back so precipitately that it banged against the wall, she saw out of the corner of her eye a small object rushing toward her, snapping at her ankles.

Since her feet were bare and unprotected, she kicked at the intruder, trying to save herself from its attack. At the time, she remembered later, she wondered how a wild animal had gotten into her house.

She grabbed the first thing that came to hand, a lamp resting on a small table, and swung it at the charging form. Her reflex was good enough to cause the blow to glance off the animal, and it howled in surprise and pain. Only at this point did she realize that it was Max, the "sweet" little dog William had presented to her the previous morning.

By this time there were four people in the minuscule hallway at the head of the stairs, and Clarissa was the only one of them who was silent. Betty was crying rather loudly, and kept insisting that she had been bitten. Lady Aria, in defense of the animal, was assuring her that she could not have been. And Meg, as late on the scene as Clarissa, was demanding in a stern voice to know what was going on.

Max howled and cowered under the table and Lady Aria, imperious as Clarissa had never seen her, insisted that she would not have her animal treated in such a fashion. She sounded frightfully like her mother.

"What is the meaning of this?" Lady Aria demanded for the third or fourth time. "You will all be discharged from my service instantly. No one, I repeat, no one is to mistreat my animal in such a manner. He is worth the lot of you."

The three other women stared at her. It was dark in the hall but none of them believed it was because Lady Aria could not see that she didn't recognize where she was—or who she was. She stamped her bare foot and thundered, "Send Kinsford to me and be quick about it! He'll have the lot of you packing before you can whistle a ditty."

With this she swung around, scooped up the little dog, who didn't dare object, and stormed back into

her room, slamming the door behind her. Meg and
Betty, wide-eyed, turned to Clarissa.

"Don't look at me," she protested. "I haven't the
slightest idea what to do. Perhaps she'll just go to
sleep and be all right when she awakens in the morning."

But this hope was instantly shattered when the
imperious voice from within the room ordered,
"Bring me a slice of gingerbread and a pot of tea.
Quickly."

"I think it would be best," Clarissa said to Meg,
"if we humor her."

"But we don't have any gingerbread."

"Well, bring her something sweet. One of the rhubarb tarts from dinner will do. I'll take it in to her,
if you don't mind."

"Not at all," Meg muttered as she pulled her robe
around her and left.

"Do you think I should go and get Lord Kinsford?" Betty asked, her brow furrowed with alarm.
"He'd want to know, I think."

"Not in the middle of the night. I won't send you
out there alone. First thing in the morning you can
send one of the village boys for him. Besides, she
isn't actually asking for this Lord Kinsford, do you
think? It sounds more like Lady Kinsford asking for
her husband, the earl's father."

Betty remained unconvinced. "You don't think it
means she's terribly sick? That we should send for
the doctor?"

Clarissa considered this, but only briefly. "No,
she's not sick in that way. At least I don't think so.
She's been disoriented before, though not quite like
this. I feel certain she'll be all right until morning."

"Should I—uh—go in there?"

"Not unless you want to be dismissed again," Clarissa said, her smile rueful. "Why don't you go to bed in Meg's room and I'll take care of Lady Aria for the rest of the night?"

"But Lord Kinsford sent me so you wouldn't have to do so much."

"Yes, but I feel responsible for Lady Aria while she's here, especially during these disoriented times. I'll call you if I need you, Betty."

The girl curtsied and disappeared into her sister's room. By the time Clarissa had managed to light a candle from her bedroom, Meg appeared with the tea and tart on a tray. Clarissa took it from her. "Go to bed," she directed her maid. "I'll call you or Betty if I need you." Meg reluctantly disappeared into her room and Clarissa stood a moment before the closed door, hearing Lady Aria's voice in monologue to the dog, not quite loud enough to be decipherable.

She rapped lightly on the door and entered without being bid, bearing the tray as both shield and enticement. "I have your tea, my lady," she said, as though it were midday and something she was accustomed to doing.

Lady Aria was propped up in bed against several pillows. She had lit her lamp and sat with the dog on her lap, talking to him in an haughty voice. It was clear she was still imitating her mother. "Put it on the table," she directed with a sweeping wave of her hand. "That doesn't look like gingerbread. I asked for gingerbread."

"There was no gingerbread," Clarissa said firmly. "You will enjoy the rhubarb tart. It was made for you especially."

"I don't like rhubarb tarts," the girl insisted, pouting. "I won't eat it. I want gingerbread."

"It's rhubarb tart or nothing," Clarissa retorted as she settled the tray on the small bedside table. Though she would have hated to see Lady Aria have a temper tantrum, she was not about to make up gingerbread in the middle of the night. "Milk and two sugars, my lady?"

"One sugar. You should know that. How long have you worked for me?"

"Some years, my lady," Clarissa admitted.

"Very unlikely. You would know how many sugars I take." Lady Aria's eyes narrowed suspiciously. "Who are you? What are you doing here?"

"I'm here to take care of you, m'lady. I think perhaps your head injury is causing you some trouble right now."

"Head injury?" Lady Aria's hand flew to her head, where she could feel the dressing above her ear. Her eyes became confused and teary. "What's happening to me?" she whispered. "What's the matter with me?"

Clarissa moved quickly to the bedside where she gently cradled Lady Aria against her shoulder. "Don't be alarmed, my dear. This is only temporary, I'm sure. You'll feel better in a few days."

"But I don't . . . know who I am. Sometimes. I forget where I am and what's happening to me." She looked up with beseeching eyes. "Can't the doctor give me something?"

"We'll speak with him tomorrow. Try to sleep now, Lady Aria. Sleep is the best healer." Clarissa helped her charge scoot down in the bed and drew the coverlet up to her chin. "I'll sleep here on the pallet. You won't be alone. Perhaps I should put the dog downstairs so he won't disturb you again.''

"No, please. He's a comfort to me.''

If not to the rest of us, Clarissa thought. But she nodded and said, "As you wish. Sleep well, my dear.''

12

When Clarissa could not get comfortable on the pallet, she spent the remainder of the night seated in the rocking chair near Lady Aria's bed. In the event of a recurrence of the girl's behavior, neither Meg nor Betty would have had the necessary authority to restrain her effectively. So Clarissa assumed the responsibility and spent a fair amount of time trying to puzzle out what was happening. She was deeply troubled by Lady Aria's behavior.

And yet she was not completely convinced that the problem was medical, that the blow to Aria's head had caused some structural damage that impinged on her brain. That was quite possible, of course. Dr. Lawrence seemed to think it likely, if Lady Aria were to remain disoriented.

Perhaps the accident had precipitated some problem. Clarissa had been in charge of Lady Aria's tutoring for the last year, and she had witnessed fluctuations of mood, but these seemed perfectly normal for a girl of Aria's age and lively disposition. Laughter and excitement and flares of temper. Occasional blue devils that would bring tears to her eyes as she did watercolors. "It was just so sad," she once explained. "The leaves were falling, it was autumn, everything was dying." And sure enough, in her picture would be leaves scattered on the faded grass, and blowing in the autumn breezes past a church and graveyard.

Not that Lady Aria was frequently downcast. More often she was in tearing spirits, full of so much energy there seemed not enough of an outlet for it. When William wasn't at home, she had a hard time finding someone to accompany her on wild gallops across the fields. The other girls in the neighborhood were not usually up to such unladylike pursuits, though they were fond enough of her that they didn't bear tales to their parents.

What concerned Clarissa now was the possibility that Lady Aria's distress might have something to do with her mother's strange behavior. After all, Lady Kinsford was downright peculiar in her habits. Could one inherit such a tendency? Could an accident precipitate it?

Heavy-eyed, Clarissa went to her room when Betty arrived to relieve her at first light. Lady Aria still slept and the dog remained curled against her back. There had been no further disturbance, from girl or dog. After penning a note to be sent to the earl, Clarissa gratefully fell on her bed and slept for a whole hour before Meg came to help her dress. She chose a drab-colored bombazine round dress with endless buttons at the back. When Meg attempted to enlivened this with a peach-colored handkerchief, Clarissa objected.

"But for the earl, ma'am," Meg protested, her fingers darting about the piece of cloth, tucking, pulling, rolling, fluffing. "*Much* better," Meg said, standing back. "And your kid half-boots instead of those slippers, if you'll allow me to say so, Miss Driscoll." She held the boots out determinedly to her mistress until, with a sigh, Clarissa took them.

"It's not as if he's going to notice what I'm wearing," Clarissa protested as she pulled them on. "Dr. Lawrence would probably pay more attention."

"Still . . ."

Clarissa sat down at the dressing table and regarded herself in the glass while Meg went to retrieve her hairbrush from Aria's room. Her oval face looked back at her from the mirror, tired smudges under the gray eyes. She groaned and touched the puffiness as though her fingers might absorb it and make it go away. "How awful! He'll think I'm totally unfit to take care of his sister," she muttered to herself as she let Meg brush her hair into its usual tidy wrap.

"I could do something different with your hair." Meg allowed the wavy brown mass to fall forward around Clarissa's face. "Soft ringlets distract the eye from the face. I've read that in the ladies' magazines."

"Just do it the usual way, Meg. It doesn't matter."

Meg snorted, and obeyed.

Lord Kinsford arrived before Clarissa had finished her toilette. Betty came up to her room and stuck her head around the door. "I've told him Lady Aria is still asleep and have put him in the sitting room. He wanted to know what happened but I told him you were the one to explain. I offered him a cup of tea, but he refused. I can hear him in there pacing about the room."

"Thank you, Betty." Before going downstairs, Clarissa checked on Lady Aria once more. The girl continued to sleep soundly, but at the sound of the opening door, Max jumped down from the bed and came to her, wagging his tail gaily as though nothing untoward had occurred during the night. As she closed the door behind them, Clarissa muttered to him, "You really are the most incomprehensible fellow. Come along. Meg will feed you and let you out."

He trotted after her down the stairs without so much as a yip of excitement. She started to lead him into the kitchen, but the sitting-room door flew open and Lord Kinsford regarded her with astonishment. "Surely the dog can wait!" he protested. "I need to know what has happened to Aria."

"Lord Kinsford, I'll be with you in a matter of moments. I'm just taking Max to the kitchen. Aria is fine right now; she's sleeping, as I'm sure Betty told you." Clarissa slipped through the door into the dining parlor, leaving him behind. She could understand his anxiety, but there were certain things that required her attention so briefly that it would have been foolhardy to ignore them. Shrugging off a feeling of guilt, she handed Max over to Meg with a request that he be fed and walked.

"But what about your breakfast, Miss Driscoll? You haven't eaten."

"I'll get something later. No, bring me tea in the sitting room after you've finished with Max, please. I'm starving." Then a thought occurred to her and she added, "The earl may not have had breakfast, either. Just set up for two in the dining parlor, if you will."

He was standing by the window when she arrived. The day outside was misty and he appeared to stare out toward the lane without interest. When he heard her tread, he turned abruptly from his contemplation and faced her. Clarissa thought he looked almost apologetic, but he said, "Your note said there had been an upsetting occurrence during the night, that Aria's mind had become disoriented again."

Clarissa seated herself and, though he hesitated, he followed suit. "The dog caused a disturbance. Barking and nipping at all our ankles for a while. I don't know what caused him to do that, and afterwards he was quite all right. He didn't actually break any skin, and certainly never tried to hurt Lady Aria. Perhaps he was protecting her."

"I really will have to speak to Will about the dog," he said. "There's something going on that obviously isn't quite right. He told me something . . ." His frown gave way to an exasperated sigh. "Right now Aria is more important. Tell me what happened."

"She suddenly became very imperious, telling us that we were all dismissed from her service. She sounded exactly like, well, if you will pardon me, your lordship, she sounded exactly like her mother."

He stiffened in his chair. "Have you ever seen my stepmother behave in that fashion?"

"No, but it's no secret in the village. She dismisses servants right and left. Fortunately, they all know that she forgets what she's done in a few hours, so they just lie low until the whole thing blows over. Otherwise, you'd have an incredible change in staff every few days at the Hall."

Kinsford seemed particularly distressed. Whether this was because she had presumed to tell tales on her betters, or because he wasn't aware of the phenomenon she was describing, Clarissa could not know. "In any case," she continued, "Lady Aria retired to her room, demanding gingerbread and tea. She wasn't happy when Meg produced a rhubarb tart, but it was all we had. She asked that 'Kinsford' be sent to her, but it was clear to me that she was referring to the late earl, and not yourself."

"Why was it so clear to you?" he asked, leaning toward her.

"Because she was, in effect, your stepmother at the time. And she was asking for her husband."

"My father has been dead for many years, Miss Driscoll. Aria would not be asking for him, even if she thought she was her mother, which sounds totally bizarre in any case."

Clarissa tried to be patient. "It was as though she were portraying a scene she'd witnessed long ago, perhaps as a child. Only now she was taking the part of her mother. She was not herself, Lord Kinsford."

"In other words, this is rather a different kind of disorientation than you've seen before."

"Yes." She rubbed her temples to soothe the aching that had begun there. "The other times she has at least been herself, though not in the appropriate time. This time she was a different person in a different time."

"You can't be sure of that."

Agitated, Clarissa rose with a dismissive gesture. "No, I can't be sure of it. But I know she didn't think she was Lady Aria because, better than you, *I* know who Lady Aria is."

Kinsford had risen almost as rapidly as she. He stood over her, glaring. Then, just as swiftly, frowning. "You look fagged to death," he said. "Didn't you get any sleep?"

His empathy completely threw her off balance, as did the finger he reached out to touch the smudge under one eye. She was, suddenly, reminded of the kiss by the stile, and a faint flush came into her cheeks. She stepped back and his finger fell away. "I sat up with your sister."

"But I sent Betty to do that."

"Neither Betty nor Meg was in a position to deal with Lady Aria in her condition last night. When I reminded her of her head injury, she soon returned to normal; only frightened, poor child. She hasn't awoken yet this morning. I think she'll be herself when she does."

He stood staring at her for a long moment. Vines scraped against the panes and wind buffeted the corner of the cottage. He *could* not be remembering the kiss. He had forgotten it the moment after it happened, Clarissa felt certain of that. And yet, he looked at her in such a way that she could almost believe he, too, was recalling that episode.

Nonsense! she scolded herself. He was undoubtedly planning how best to handle the situation with his sister and wasn't aware that his gaze had remained on her. Only when there was a tap at the door and Meg entered did his gaze shift.

"Lady Aria is awake now," she announced. "She seems to be all right." This was for Clarissa's benefit, and was supposed to carry a certain significance which not only the two of them but Lord Kinsford understood: Their patient was not, at present, crazy as a loon. Meg carried a tray with tea and an assortment of foods which she set down on the table near the sofa. "I've taken some breakfast up for her and told her that the earl is here."

"Thank you, Meg." Clarissa indicated the food with an expansive gesture. "We thought you might not have eaten, Lord Kinsford. Won't you join me?"

He hesitated briefly, as though he would go to Lady Aria first, and then nodded. "She'll need time to eat her own meal without interruption," he said, as if in explanation. When they were both seated and Meg had left, he asked, "What did you mean when you said you knew Aria better than I do?"

It was a question Clarissa was uncertain how to answer. She poured a cup of tea for each of them, and spread jam on a scone. "I see her several times a week, Lord Kinsford. Because you're very seldom at the Hall, you haven't had the opportunity to get to know your brother and sister."

"But I've known them all their lives. You underestimate my interest and my concern." He chose the veal-and-ham pie with a muffin and marmalade. Before taking a bite, however, he added, "I do not take my responsibility for the children lightly."

"Hmmm. I can see you believe that, and yet you spend so little time here. Children change, and their needs change." She waved aside his attempted protest. "Forgive me. I don't wish to quarrel with you, sir. Certainly not over breakfast. Let us say that you are showing a decided concern for your sister in her illness."

"I'm always concerned for both Aria and Will. I have obligations in London as well. Matters of state can be very pressing."

Clarissa regarded him over the rim of her teacup. "Matters of state," she said, replacing the cup on the table, "can be an excellent excuse for doing precisely what one wishes. In your case, that might include not residing in the country with a rather odd stepmama and two charming though undisciplined half-siblings.''

His eyes flashed. ''I suppose this is more of your plain speaking, Miss Driscoll. And that you think it is perfectly acceptable for you to speak in such a fashion on behalf of your charges.''

Clarissa replied with a calmness that was meant to defuse the situation. ''Please don't misunderstand me, Lord Kinsford. I'm not criticizing you. I wouldn't, in your place, be any more anxious to spend time in the country than you are, I dare say. You can see that William and Lady Aria are delightful children and it must seem to you that they go on perfectly well without your guidance. Unfortunately, that's not quite true.''

''One doesn't have to be on the scene every minute to give guidance. Plenty of other children manage perfectly well without their guardians living on top of them.''

''William has been sent down from school, and there's very little for him to do in the country except get into trouble,'' she pointed out. ''Please, believe me that I understand the demands on you in town. And I realize you think I have no right speaking to you this way. I suppose I shouldn't do it, and I probably wouldn't if I weren't so concerned for both of them. Perhaps you could take your brother to live with you in town, take him under your wing, as it were. He's just at the age when that would be most useful.''

Kinsford was obviously struggling to match her reasonableness. ''I've thought of having him there with me, but think of the trouble he could get up to in London! Gambling, drinking, women, there's no end to the vices he could indulge."

Clarissa raised her eyebrows in astonishment. "Surely you aren't suggesting that the boy has to behave better than you did at his age! You were hardly a paragon of virtue, Kinsford! You can't keep him away from the metropolis forever. With or without your patronage, he's going to make it there eventually. Is it that you would be bored with guiding such a pup?"

"As you have so kindly pointed out," he observed as he carefully set down his knife, "I am hardly the best person to demand perfect behavior from my brother."

"He doesn't have to behave perfectly." Clarissa leaned toward him, earnestness softening her face. "He's just a youngster. He's full of high spirits and basically sound judgment. You have only to guide him to the best of your ability. Show him how to go on. Interest him in some endeavors that will use his energy and his time; give him a chance to feel productive. You know, Kinsford, what finally brought you around was not your father's harangues or your mother's tears. It was your experience in the military and finding afterwards that politics interested you, and that you were good at it."

Stung, Kinsford said, "I think, Miss Driscoll, that your reproofs are somewhat misplaced." He was not accustomed to being spoken to in such a fashion, especially not by someone who had rather shaky claims to proper behavior. "I'm perfectly capable of managing my brother without your assistance. I have already arranged with Alman to have Will start learning estate business in all earnestness, both to keep him occupied and to prepare him for his future. And, in due course, I intend to see that he gets the proper town polish that every young man needs.''

"It sounds a splendid program for William," she acknowledged with a warm smile. "I only meant to suggest . . . "

But Kinsford was not finished. "I fail to understand how you, a spinster without husband or children, have come to regard yourself as such an authority on how young people should be raised. Perhaps as a substitute for never having married, you have adopted my family's concerns as your own.''

Astonished, Clarissa stared at him. "I assure you I'm perfectly content with my way of life, Kinsford, and I do not claim any expertise in raising children. Lady Aria and William, however, have undoubtedly needed some guidance and I would be the first to applaud your decision to offer them yours.''

Chagrined at her ready acquiescence, since he was now in the mood to do battle, Kinsford pressed her on yet another subject. "And I do not believe for one moment that such a woman as Lorelia Snolgrass exists, and that if she does, I doubt very much if you have ever laid eyes upon her!''

A laugh was startled out of Clarissa, who demurely lowered her eyes. "Now how can you suspect such a thing, Lord Kinsford? In all these years no one else has seen fit to question her existence.''

"There was no hairbrush in your room," he replied succinctly.

"Ah, yes, I should never have allowed you in my bedchamber," she murmured, her lips quivering.

He was unable to resist her teasing and a grin dispersed his darker mood. "But I'm right, am I not?" he insisted.

"Of course. Aren't you always?"

Kinsford sighed. "I'm not so sure. I should go see Aria now," he said, and with a half-bow left the room.

13

Kinsford's tap at Aria's door was answered immediately and he let himself in to find his sister sitting up in bed with a tray across her legs. She had eaten most of her breakfast, but put down her spoon when he entered.

"Don't frown so, Alexander," she begged him. "I was not myself in the night. You know I wouldn't have spoken to anyone in that fashion if I'd been myself."

"But you remember doing it?" he asked, taking the rocking chair beside her bed. "It's not something that disappears from your mind when you become yourself again?"

Aria shuddered extravagantly. "I wish I *could* forget doing it. Oh, Kinsford, it's so frightening." She burst into tears, her whole body shaking with sobs.

Kinsford removed the tray, setting it on the floor before he slipped onto the edge of the bed and put his arm around her shoulders. "My dear child, of course you're frightened. You're afraid something has happened to your mind, that the accident has somehow damaged it. I don't think it has, Aria. Most of the time you're perfectly all right."

He stroked the hair back from her forehead where it lay pressed against his shoulder. He wasn't sure he was telling her the truth. He was telling her what he wanted to believe, but not perhaps what he feared in his own heart.

In a voice broken by hiccoughs, Aria said, "I don't know when it's going to happen. It just does. I'll think at the time that what I'm saying and doing is perfectly normal. And then, a few minutes later, when Miss Driscoll reminds me of where I am, and who I am, I know it was all wrong."

Her voice dropped to a whisper. "And each time it's been a little worse, hasn't it? Oh, Meg and Betty were so upset about it. I could see it in their faces this morning. Only Miss Driscoll seems to accept what's happening without a blink of her eyes. She's been so very kind to me." She pressed his arm and added fervently, "I hope you've thanked her for everything she's doing."

"I'm sure I have," he said dubiously.

Aria's eyes pooled up again. "Oh, Alexander, you aren't still unhappy with Miss Driscoll, are you?"

Evasively, he replied, "I think we should move you up to the Hall."

His sister pushed away from his comforting shoulder, a look of confusion on her face. "But . . . but the ride. It might jar me. And cause my condition to worsen. Mightn't it?"

He regarded her intently for a long moment. "It's only a precaution, keeping you here. I think you would tolerate the ride very well."

Aria leaned back against the pillows and turned her gaze to the window. Outside were the twitterings of birds and the swaying of vines, the sky now blue and scattered with plump white clouds. Without looking at Kinsford, she confessed, "I feel safe here, Alexander. Safer than I think I would be at the Hall.

I don't . . . actually want to come home, until I've learned what's happening.''

Kinsford was stunned. ''Don't want to come home?'' he repeated, incredulous. ''But Aria, we have every comfort there, and your own family around you, and any number of servants to provide for your needs.''

''But I feel safe with Miss Driscoll and Meg.''

''I think you're being unduly influenced by your illness. Surely you would feel just as safe at Kinsford Hall.''

A tear trickled down Aria's cheek. ''Miss Driscoll is my friend. She *understands* me. Even if it turns out to be something horrid, she'll understand and accept it.''

''But so would we, your family.''

Aria looked down at her folded hands, and slowly shook her head. ''Not in the same way. You would want to. You would try to. But think of Mama. She would make such a scene about it, and carry on. And Will would be so upset that he wouldn't be able to act normally with me. And you.''

A painful little smile lifted her lips. ''You would think of all the consequences, and make plans for them, as if you were carrying a bill through the Lords. I would be something that required serious thought and close attention. You would see to it that I had the very best care.'' Another tear slid down her cheek and she brushed it away with a knuckle. ''But you wouldn't *be* there. You would have other things to do. Important things.''

''Aria, I care very deeply about you.''

''I know you do. But Miss Driscoll is here. And she's going to stay here. And she accepts me in a way no one else quite does. Maybe it's because she *isn't* family, and she still loves me for myself."

"I love you for yourself, too, Aria."

"Yes, but you don't know me very well, do you?" She laid her hand over his, as though he were the one who needed comforting. "It's all right, Alexander. I know you'll take care of me. I just need to stay here until I know what's happening to me. Can you see that?"

"I suppose so," he lied.

"Thank you, Alexander. For understanding."

He didn't understand, of course. He didn't seem to have understood one damn thing that was going on since he'd returned to the Hall. By the time he left Miss Driscoll's cottage, pulling the door to behind himself with slightly unnecessary vigor, the Earl of Kinsford would gladly have retreated to his comfortable, impregnable home in London if it had been at all possible.

It was not Aria and her illness, or Will and his problems, or his stepmother and her oddities, that most disturbed the earl at that moment, however. It was the growing realization that Miss Driscoll had come to play a large role in his family. Dismiss this as he might to the woman herself, it made her influence no less powerful.

Worse, he was becoming disturbingly attracted to her. Clarissa Driscoll, whom he had kissed at a stile one glorious spring day when they were young, seemed to hold a renewed fascination for him. He hadn't intended, even then, to let her slip from his life. But he and his father were at loggerheads constantly at that period of his life, which made it impossible for him to continue to live at Kinsford Hall.

He left with regret for only Clarissa. And in the

excitement of his new military life, thoughts of her were forced to the back of his mind. Or, occasionally, she was the woman of his fantasies. Not the real Clarissa, of course. Not the woman who became a spinster and taught pianoforte to young ladies. That woman he hadn't known, with her fierce independence and determination and idiosyncrasies.

Mounting Longbridge with absentminded ease, Kinsford admitted to himself that he hadn't wanted to know her. The reality of the situation was too complicated. She might very well blame his family for her severely reduced circumstances. She had never made any attempt to draw his attention or to ask for his assistance. He had a life in London that required great amounts of his time and energies. It just hadn't made sense to get to know her.

Until now.

Clarissa had a long talk with Dr. Lawrence. He had shaken his head ruefully as he said, "Who is to doubt that Lady Kinsford might have produced a child with an oddity or two? I've seen it happen more than once. I tend to believe, however, that the present behavior must have some relation to the accident."

He regarded Clarissa solemnly for a moment, pressing her hand in a kindly fashion. "My prescription for you, my dear ma'am, is some fresh air and a long nap. Promise me you'll take care of yourself."

"I promise," Clarissa agreed.

Aria seemed rather subdued when Clarissa went up to check on her, but perfectly normal. Relieved, she crawled into her own bed and slept until late in the afternoon.

* * *

Lord Kinsford arrived in the early evening bearing hampers of food. He had sent a note to Aria advising her to expect this largess, and to advise Miss Driscoll and her household help of there being no necessity to prepare the evening meal. Aria was delighted by the possibility of Kinsford and Miss Driscoll sharing a meal in such a friendly fashion and joined them in the dining parlor in spirits that she attempted to tone down a bit for the occasion.

Looking around the table at the joint of cold roast beef, the roast duck, the pigeon pie, the basket of salad, the stewed fruit, the pastry biscuits, the cheesecake and the plum pudding, Aria exclaimed, "You have done us proud, Kinsford. Mrs. Stalker knows how to prepare a picnic better than anyone on earth! Did you bring wine?"

Her brother regarded her ruefully. "Are you sure you're not well, Aria?" At the stricken look on her face, he instantly repented his teasing. "I've brought it to tempt you, and Miss Driscoll, of course. And yes, I've brought wine, though I'm not at all sure whether it would be good for you. I brought lemonade."

He turned with a politely questioning look to Clarissa. "Oh, I daresay the wine will do her no harm," she said. "She assures me she has quite tired of ginger beer and lemonade."

"Mama allows me wine with my evening meal," Aria informed her brother. "I am, after all, fifteen years of age."

"Oh, ancient," he laughed. "However, I feel certain I was drinking ale and claret at fifteen, so how can I deny you such a treat?"

Kinsford poured wine for each of them in crystal

glasses he had brought from the Hall. Lifting his glass in a toast, he said, "To Lady Aria's quick return to perfect health. "His companions gladly drank to that, though Lady Aria's eyes sparkled rather suspiciously in the candlelight even before she'd had a sip of the wine.

Aria watched with pride as her brother provided charming dinner table conversation, his topics ranging wide over the spectrum of politics, society and country matters. Aria thought Miss Driscoll seemed to particularly enjoy this display, and when Kinsford called on Miss Driscoll to participate in the exchange, explaining where she had herself learned the pianoforte, drawing, and voice, she readily accommodated him with delightful tales of a companion who sang in the schoolroom at night, and a drawing master who occasionally used his neckcloth to wipe off his paint brushes.

Even as Aria was laughing over this last episode, she saw Kinsford lean back slightly in his chair, having almost finished with his meal, and observe Miss Driscoll with a mixture of playfulness and curiosity on his strong features. "And do I take it that it is your very own Miss Snolgrass who acquaints you with the latest dance steps? Does she pick them up in her wanderings?"

Clarissa, mellow from the wine and easy companionship at the table, incautiously admitted to the truth. "Oh, no. Lorelia has no interest in dance steps at all. It is Steven who has a remarkable facility for picking up the latest dances. Bath is the ideal place to discover what is new, if one cannot be in London."

Kinsford's brows had lowered alarmingly. "You mean he teaches you the steps here, in your house?"

The tone of his voice alerted Aria instantly to his extreme disapproval. Recklessly, she interjected, "Well, how else is Miss Driscoll to learn the steps, Alexander? She never goes anywhere. They must come to her."

Her elders were not distracted by her attempted reason. Kinsford was regarding Clarissa with flashing eyes, and she returned his gaze with cool imperturbability. They were locked in this pose for several minutes.

"How close a relative *is* Mr. Traling?" he finally inquired.

Clarissa looked disposed to refuse an answer to this question, but Aria pleaded silently with her to speak. With a sigh, Clarissa said, "He's a second cousin. One of my few living relatives. He should have inherited at least a nominal share of Pennhurst, as the only living male. My father left both of us rather stranded."

Aria breathed her relief. *No one* could possibly see anything wrong in such a connection. Rather the reverse. There was every reason for Miss Driscoll and Mr. Traling to share this painful burden of being dispossessed. Aria turned to Kinsford, expecting to find him satisfied. But his frown remained. Nevertheless, he picked up the thread of a former piece of conversation, elaborating quite unnecessarily on the management of his succession houses, as he proceeded to finish his meal.

This confused Aria. She knew Kinsford wasn't happy, but he obviously intended to say no more about the matter of the dancing instruction. Aria quite liked the idea of Miss Driscoll and Mr. Traling waltzing about the sitting room of Miss Driscoll's cottage, with perhaps Miss Driscoll herself hum-

ming some Viennese waltz as they swung to and fro.
When she and Will took instruction, Miss Driscoll
played the pianoforte and hummed as well.

After a while Kinsford turned to his sister and said,
"You seem to have eaten your fill, my dear. And
you are looking quite tired. Perhaps you had best go
up and climb into your bed. The last thing I intended
was to overtire you."

Though she was indeed exhausted, it was not this
which determined her to obey her brother on this
occasion. With a quick smile of thanks to Clarissa,
and an instruction for her brother to come to her
later, after his port, she meekly let herself out of the
dining parlor, (almost) closing the door carefully behind her. She would be able to see Miss Driscoll,
but not her brother from her vantage point outside
the room. She would, however, be able to hear both
of them, as she clearly did now.

"How could you say that in front of my sister?"
the earl demanded, real feeling in his voice. "She's
hardly of an age to hear such disclosures."

"Such disclosures?" Clarissa repeated, incredulous. "Just what do you think I was saying, Lord
Kinsford?"

"I am referring to your dancing with your cousin,
of course. Alone, unchaperoned, a man and a
woman in each other's arms. Hardly the type of behavior one would expect from a person of your
birth."

Clarissa pushed aside her second, half-full glass
of wine. "Tell me, Kinsford, exactly what you expected me to say when you asked if Lorelia Snolgrass had taught me the dances. You knew Lorelia
didn't exist . . ."

Though Miss Driscoll continued, Aria lost track

of the conversation for a moment. Lorelia Snolgrass did not exist? But how extraordinary! And how very clever of Miss Driscoll. Really, Aria had had no idea how decidedly enterprising her instructress was. Certainly Miss Driscoll would not cavil at a little playacting on her own part.

Kinsford's thundering voice brought Aria's attention back to the scene in the dining parlor. "I expected you to say something in keeping with your Snolgrass story. To play along with the deception, because we are both aware of it now. God knows I didn't expect you to confess to improper behavior in front of a fifteen-year-old!"

"Lady Aria was perfectly satisfied with the truth of the situation," Clarissa retorted. Aria could see her shoulders shrug helplessly. "Why, to one of her age, a second cousin is quite as unremarkable as a brother, and certainly she learns her dances with Master William all the time."

Aria felt sure this was another argument which would calm the earl's excitement, but no. "He might as well be a stranger for all the propriety your dancing with him has," Kinsford insisted. "No young woman of your age could possibly believe it is acceptable behavior to do any such thing."

"There you are quite out. I most certainly do believe that I have done nothing the least bit wrong, and I will not have you judge me by some ludicrous standard of appearances. This is *my* cottage, and *my* village and I dance with *my* cousin. For God's sake, Kinsford, he's married."

"And you are a spinster!" Kinsford flung his napkin away from him in disgust. "What would happen if one of the villagers happened by your window when you and your *cousin* were dancing about, locked in an embrace? Surely you can see the damage that would do!''

Clarissa rose from her chair and stood with arms folded across her chest, glaring down at him. ''Yes, indeed, I can see it. And do you know, I do not care a whit! And you have yourself to thank for that, Kinsford. It was your example which determined me early on to pay no heed to the gossips and grumblers. What possible difference could it make if they suspected the worst? Do I have a reputation to lose? Would their shunning me be any more difficult than my losing my place in county society?''

Aria wanted to run to her and put her arms around her and protect her. Miss Driscoll, though her stance was fierce, seemed uncommonly vulnerable. Surely Kinsford would see that.

''You would know the difference soon enough,'' he retorted, rising now to stand and face her across the table, eyes narrowed. ''You would know when they cut you direct, when the good women of the village refused to speak to you. And you would certainly not have the children of the gentry pouring into your cottage for lessons.''

At length, in a flat voice, Clarissa said, ''Well, it hasn't happened. If anyone has seen me dancing with my cousin they must have written it off to my eccentricity and not my immorality, as you have. I presume they find me far too old and uninteresting to elicit such thoughts.''

''Old!'' he scoffed. ''Don't be foolish, Clarissa. You are not nearly old enough or plain enough to be free from such talk. You are merely lucky that you have so far avoided it.'' He suddenly reached across the table and touched the white cap perched on her hair. "This won't protect you. Promise me you won't let Traling visit you unchaperoned."

Clarissa reached up and tugged off the offending cap. "I cannot promise you any such thing. You don't seem to understand, Kinsford. My life is very circumscribed. I cannot and will not allow it to become any more so."

Aria felt a thrill of excitement at both of their exchanges. Something, some subtle current, was at work here but she could not precisely say what it was. Kinsford had called her Clarissa; Miss Driscoll had removed her cap. And shaken out her hair, almost as a challenge, Aria thought. And then she heard Kinsford say, in his stiffest voice, "Very well. I'd best say good night to Aria." Whereupon she dashed on tiptoe for the stairs.

14

While Lady Aria slept late the next morning, Clarissa found it difficult to stay in bed until dawn. She had been shaken by the interview with Kinsford, in several ways. Though she knew he had the weight of standard wisdom on his side, she could not see changing her habits and patterns just for the sake of appearances. On the one hand, she could lose her livelihood; on the other, her self-respect. One had to take a few risks in life to make it mean more than drudgery. And Steven. Surely he needed her support now more than ever.

Clarissa was not able to look directly at those last few moments with Lord Kinsford, when he had called her by her name. When they were young he had called her Clarissa. When he had kissed her, her name had whispered on his lips. Surely there was nothing to be made of his backhanded compliment about her age and attractiveness. Still, there had been a moment when he had seemed open to her, when he had seemed to want to reestablish that less formal relationship they'd had when they were young. He had asked her to do something for him, and she had wanted to please him. Only what he asked was too much.

Unsettled, Clarissa urged Max from his cozy spot

beside the sleeping Lady Aria. A walk would do them both good. The minute she opened the front door he started barking with delirious excitement. ''That's enough,'' she said firmly, tightening the lead so he had to walk near her. He trotted along then with the plume of his little tail waving back and forth, quite content. Clarissa let her mind drift away from the present as they traversed the lane and then the path across the fields.

She had learned, years before, how to achieve a measure of tranquility when her situation was in fact rather distressing When her father had gambled, when he had died, when she had found herself alone and frightened, she had learned to let her mind wander to a safe place, where it was always spring and she was happy. *The difference between me and Lady Kinsford,* she thought ruefully, *is that she tries to inhabit such a place all the time and I acknowledge that it's only a brief escape.* And it was easier for her to find this escape when she was outside, walking briskly around the countryside.

The blackthorn of the hedgerow was a mass of white blossoms and the delicate pink flowers of dogrose pushed their way along side of it. On the other side of the path, at the edge of the pasture, were bright yellow celandine and purplish lady's smock. A pink-breasted linnet sang atop a bright green bush.

Clarissa drank in the smell of new grass and the scent of the spring flowers. The tightness in her chest and shoulders eased as she swung along, humming softly to herself. It was a glorious day, spring was well under way, and she could believe that Lady Aria would be all right.

Max barked vigorously at a hedgehog unwise enough to show its nose at the side of the dirt path.

Instantly the prickly little animal wrapped itself into a ball and Max alternately charged and retreated, puzzled and frustrated by the alarming spines he encountered. Clarissa laughed and dragged him away. "Leave the poor creature alone, you silly animal. He's not doing you a bit of harm."

Max reluctantly allowed himself to be drawn away, with many a backward glance and yap. But he was easily distracted, and soon trotted along again sniffing at each fascinating rock and tree along the way. Clarissa covered ground rather quickly, but the dog had no difficulty keeping up with her, and was usually a little ahead. They were about to pass a rider coming toward them, and Clarissa was relieved to see that it was no one she knew, when the rider drew in his horse, frowned and said, "That's my dog."

"I beg your pardon?" Clarissa replied. She'd never seen the fellow before. He looked a rather meek sort of person, and rode with no distinction whatsoever. And yet his eyes were keen enough and he spoke quite decidedly.

"That's my dog," he repeated.

"I can't think how it could be," she answered, and yet given a moment, perhaps she could. "Cairn terriers look very similar, you know."

"Where did you get it? You haven't had him long, have you?"

Clarissa hesitated. But there was nothing for it except to admit the truth. "I was given him, only two days ago, by William Kinsford."

"Precisely!" the fellow ejaculated. "I might have known! They kidnapped him."

It was Clarissa's turn to frown. "If you would introduce yourself, sir, perhaps we could straighten out this matter," she suggested, drawing the dog close to her. Max was paying absolutely no attention to the rider, though the rider's horse seemed to intrigue him.

"I, madam, am Gerald Franklin, master at Oak Knoll, where William attends school. I am, in fact, on my way at this moment to Kinsford Hall to confront him with the stealing of my dog, Harding."

Even at this name Max did not look up at the man. Clarissa, however, had no difficulty believing that he belonged to Mr. Franklin, given his further explanation.

"A companion of William's has admitted that he was responsible for removing Harding from the school grounds and bringing him to William. I hold both boys responsible for the theft and intend to prosecute them to the fullest extent of the law."

Lord, that's just what we need now, Clarissa thought. It seemed likely to her that the master was more intent on inducing Lord Kinsford to part with some money, but that was the earl's problem. She would only further irritate him, and rightly so, if she interfered in the matter.

She looked down at Max/Harding and sighed. Well, she hadn't really wanted a dog to begin with, she reminded herself. "Shall I hand him up to you?" she asked.

The master glowered. It was obvious he hadn't considered the possibility that he would have to cart the little dog around. "I suppose you'd best," he replied. "Lord Kinsford just might not believe me if I don't have the evidence. What's your name, madam?"

"Clarissa Driscoll." She reached down and lifted the curious dog, who licked her face. When she handed him up to the rider, Max cocked his head and barked. Without thanking her, Mr. Franklin rode off, awkwardly shifting the little dog on his lap, where Max squirmed and growled.

"Be still!" she heard the man say as he cuffed the little dog smartly. Clarissa shook her head, feeling all the beauty, safety and comfort of her walk disintegrate around her. Slowly, missing all the signs of spring now, she retraced her steps home.

Lord Kinsford did not return to Kinsford Hall until an hour after Mr. Franklin arrived. The school master had been shown into a waiting area off the main hall, a small room with a modicum of comforts which was not intended to inspire long waits or overly long conversations. Since Mr. Franklin had not vouchsafed to the staff what his purpose was in seeking out Lord Kinsford, other than to say that he was from William's school, no one had thought it necessary to track down the earl, as he was due back in a short while.

Kinsford returned from a strenuous ride on Longbridge (occasioned by his extreme agitation concerning Miss Driscoll), only to be greeted with the news that someone awaited him. As he had ridden past the house, he'd remarked the stranger standing in the tall window where petitioners were placed against his return. There was nothing Kinsford wanted less than to see someone with a demand upon his time and good nature just then. Nor did he like the looks of the fellow, dressed almost entirely in black, a morbid vision at best.

So it was in less than the best temper that he presented himself in the waiting area, not bothering to change from his riding clothes. The first thing that struck him as strange was the presence of the dog.

And that it was a cairn terrier. Mr. Franklin wore a stern, unrelenting grimace, and an old-fashioned set of knee breeches and jacket so reminiscent of a clergyman that Kinsford had to remind himself that this man was from Oak Knoll, not a parish church.

Oak Knoll was a family tradition, a school chosen more for its proximity than its status. None of the Barringtons for the last few generations had been particularly academically inclined, and father to son there had been an understanding that the rigors of Eton were not to be borne by them, with its hazing and stifling regulation. Oak Knoll drew from the gentry in the western portion of Britain, and had nothing to apologize for in the education it handed down, but it was a little more lenient than some of the more prestigious schools. Which was an important factor, since most of the Barrington males had been of a wild and rambunctious nature.

Kinsford introduced himself and shook hands with the master, waving him to a straight-backed chair and taking another for himself. "I understand you're from Oak Knoll," he said, ignoring the dog, since he felt sure the master would get around to the terrier in his own good time.

"I have never, myself, had William as a student," Mr. Franklin said, "though I understand he is not much of a scholar from masters who have. Oak Knoll, unfortunately, does not have the most rigorous academic standards for our students. There is a philosophy of almost indifference to such excellence, which is a great disappointment to those of us who cherish the caliber of student so popular at Eton and Harrow. Perhaps you yourself went to one of the more renowned schools."

"I went to Oak Knoll, as my father did before me," Kinsford replied.

"I see."

Max had had enough of his unaccustomed role as a quiet, retiring pet. The moment he sensed Franklin's distraction, he leaped down from the master's lap and jumped up into Kinsford's, barking excitedly and attempting to lick the earl's face. Kinsford, who felt this placed him in an undignified position, grasped the dog around the waist and lifted him to the floor. "Stay!" he commanded and, surprisingly, Max cocked his head at him, squatted down on his haunches, and stayed.

"It's about the dog I've come," Mr. Franklin said, frowning at the animal but making no attempt to issue his own ultimatum. "He was stolen from me by your brother, William."

The thought that had been drifting through Kinsford's mind for the past two days finally jelled. He could remember, quite clearly, Will's story about absconding with the dog that snapped at the students as they hurried to classes. He was certain that the boys had returned the animal at the time.

"My brother was sent down two weeks ago. I don't think he could possibly have had the dog hidden here for all that time."

"William may not have actually taken the animal this time," the master admitted, adding, "though he certainly did once before. But as you can clearly see, the animal is here and Miss Driscoll informed me that she had been given the dog by William."

"How did you know Miss Driscoll had the dog?"

"I didn't," the master said, smirking. "I happened to see her walking the animal when I was riding here and I knew Harding at once, of course.

I've had him for two years and I could tell him from a whole pack of cairn terriers, were the necessity to arise.''

This was issued as something of a challenge, Kinsford suspected, and he suspected also that, were he able to round up a few other cairn terriers, the master would not have the least idea which of them was his. It was a bluff which he would have loved to have called, but he couldn't for the life of him think of another animal of the breed in the neighborhood. Probably Mr. Franklin surmised something of the sort, having seen only the farm dogs and hunting breeds most common to the area on his ride through.

"Since my brother hasn't been away from the area since he was sent down, how could he have come by the animal?" Kinsford reiterated.

"I am convinced that this friend Upton brought the dog here to him. He had permission to go home overnight because of an ailing parent. Ha! These children think we're stupid. As if we couldn't figure out who had gone where, and why! He brought the dog here, of course. Miss Driscoll said she had only received the animal two days ago from William. Which proves my point!''

The man sat on his uncomfortable chair in splendid self-righteousness. Kinsford wished he could kick him out of the Hall and dismiss the matter, but of course that wasn't possible. He sighed and admitted, "I imagine you're correct in assuming that Mr. Upton brought the dog to William, and that my brother in turn gave the dog to Miss Driscoll, although it is not a certainty. Tell me, Mr. Franklin, can you think of a reason they would wish to take your dog away from you?''

The man flushed slightly, even as he waved aside

the question. "It cannot possibly matter why they stole the animal. The fact is that they did, and that I am prepared to prosecute William to the fullest extent of the law. These young people cannot be allowed to steal and have the world dismiss it as a boy's prank."

"And yet, as a master at a boys' school, I dare say you could recognize it as exactly that," the earl mused. "The boys, dressed for chapel, wearing their long gowns, find themselves attacked by a small dog each day as they hurry by. In fact, the very same thing happened last night at Miss Driscoll's house, I understand. My sister, who has suffered a concussion and cannot be moved, was asleep at Miss Driscoll's house when the dog Max started barking and snapping at the maid in her night robe. It was a very upsetting occurrence for the four women, alone in the house with what they must have thought was a mad dog." Kinsford nodded slowly. "Yes, I can quite see how anyone would become distressed with the small creature, and, of course, with his owner."

Kinsford made certain not to look down at Max at this point, as the "mad" dog was gazing devotedly at him, as friendly and eager to please as a puppy. Mr. Franklin, however, was not moved by Kinsford's revelation of the previous night's incident nor by his logic.

"Harding may snap occasionally at an errant student. He is not a vicious dog, as the headmaster at Oak Knoll would tell you himself. In defense of his territory he can sound fierce. He is a particularly precious dog to me, and I feel that William must be held accountable for his actions."

"What do you propose to do?"

"I will put my case before the local magistrate."
He looked inquiringly at Lord Kinsford for a name.

"Sir John Herbert."

"These local magistrates are often tired of the
shenanigans of the neighborhood boys and I'm sure
he would see that William was properly punished."

"Did you have in mind for him to be hung, or
merely transported?" Kinsford inquired with bright-
eyed interest.

"Hung?" Mr. Franklin stared at him. "Well, of
course not. He should have to pay damages for his
action. Though my dog has now been restored to
me, I have suffered severely from his loss."

"Were you planning to hold Mr. Upton responsible as well?"

Franklin shifted uneasily in his seat. "It's no use
bringing him up before a magistrate. He's incorri-
gible, and he's on scholarship."

"I see." Kinsford had felt certain they were bar-
gaining over money, but it was useful to have this
confirmed. "You'll find Sir John located just the
other side of Pennwick, maybe a mile down the lane
to Corston. On the right, a large house with an entry
lane of larches. He's accustomed to handling matters
quickly, so he'll probably arrange for a hearing on
the issue within a few days.

"Days? I would have to insist that the matter be
settled immediately, tomorrow at the latest. I have
my responsibilities at school to attend to."

Kinsford stroked his chin and mused, "He'll want
to have Will there. It would hardly be fair to hold a
hearing without him being able to defend himself. I
imagine Will would have something to say about the
reasons for the dog's abduction. Possibly even wish
to hold his owner (yourself) responsible for endan-

gering students and creating a disturbance of the peace. Yes, definitely William must have his say."

Franklin looked less certain than he had previously. But he straightened his shoulders and rasped, "Our English magistrates have a reputation for integrity which I'm sure your Sir John will wish to uphold."

Kinsford nodded. "Indeed. Sir John will be desirous of doing the right thing, especially as he is my brother's godfather." This was not *precisely* true. Sir John was actually Kinsford's own godfather, but he and Lady Herbert frequently referred to themselves as godparents to all the fourth earl's children. Who was to quibble with such a small distortion of the truth? He was obviously learning a few tricks from Clarissa Driscoll.

Defeated, Franklin turned acid. "That's just like the aristocracy, to use their position to abuse the little fellow," he hissed. "Well, I shall see that your brother is not invited back to Oak Knoll. I have that much power."

Kinsford doubted it, but it was not his intent to send the master off in a rage. "You misunderstand me," he interjected smoothly. "I had intended to send William to you to see if you could not reach a suitable arrangement without the necessity of involving Sir John. Would that be satisfactory?"

His dignity somewhat restored, Franklin murmured a cursory agreement.

"Then I'll send my brother to you," Kinsford said as he rose. When Max attempted to follow him from the room, he ordered the dog to stay and, looking puzzled, the little animal did so.

In his study, he explained the situation to William. "I shall allow you to handle the matter, Will. He is obviously more interested in money than in the animal, and your sister is inordinately fond of the dog. Pay him something for the little beast and I'll take it from your allowance." As the boy prepared to leave he added, "And, Will, you should apologize, you know. Despite the fact that the man is obnoxious, you and your friend Upton have indeed harmed him."

To Kinsford's surprise, Will nodded. "Trust me, Kinsford. I can handle it."

"I know you can."

A while later Kinsford watched from his window as the master stalked over to his horse and mounted. William followed with the dog tucked under his arm and waited until Franklin had ridden out of sight. Then, catching Kinsford's eye, he indicated that he was off to the village to return Max.

The earl dusted a spattering of dirt from his buckskin breeches. Surely it was easier to manage the affairs of state than to keep track of one small household in the country! he thought ruefully. And yet, for the first time, he realized that his family duties did not weigh so burdensomely on him as he had expected. There was a challenge here of a different type, but of no less interest than that in London.

Not that he intended to stay here forever. When Aria was well, he would return to the capital. He had only to make arrangements for her safekeeping—a governess, perhaps, or a companion. Or she could return to school, a new one if the old was impossible. Definitely there were arrangements that could be made. And he would come home more regularly to oversee the household. It could be done, and with no damage to his brother and sister, surely.

There was, however, the matter of Clarissa Driscoll. That was not so easily to be resolved. If he took the children from her care, he could impoverish her, and he would not do that. Yet how could he not remove his sister from the care of someone who refused to bend to the demands of convention? Clarissa's situation seemed to him to be a scandal waiting to happen.

Though his father had been to some degree responsible for her coming down in the world, Kinsford knew he could never right that wrong, could not make up for her years of barely scraping by, and suspected that Clarissa would not welcome any highhanded interference from him. And yet he would have to do something. Set up a trust fund for her, or offer her an interest-free mortgage. So there would be no nonsense about a dame school. Preposterous! She was not cut out to be run ragged by a bunch of undisciplined village and farm children.

He was not as yet ready to examine his own feelings for the woman. He had never been long enough in the country to feel the pull that she exerted on him, until now. His youthful fantasies had seemed just that, too childish to contemplate. He was a mature, responsible member of the House of Lords, with no time for romantic memories.

And besides, Clarissa wasn't like that any more. She wasn't the sweet, charming young girl he had known. She was strong and opinionated and dismissive of his natural claims to formality and respect. She was attractive still, to be sure, but hardly the fresh-faced beauty of the past. She was, in short, a woman. And one to be reckoned with—unintimidated by him, unimpressed by his title or even his position of influence, unwilling to bend even before his ability to deprive her of the majority of her income.

Not that he would ever have been able to treat her so shabbily. But what the devil was he to do about her?

15

Clarissa had to admit to a certain amount of pleasure when William showed up with Max again, explaining that he had had no difficulty in getting Mr. Franklin to sell him the dog. "Especially after I apologized to him for all the trouble I'd caused," he explained, adding with twinkling eyes, "And intimated that a cairn terrier was not a *manly* sort of dog and that Max would do better with my sister." Whereupon he had proudly borne the dog forth to Aria, whose delighted cries Clarissa could hear even in the sitting room.

Shortly after William departed, the Earl of Kinsford presented himself, obviously determined to be pleasant. "No doubt Will has told you the whole story," he said, as he seated himself in the chair she indicated beside the sofa. "I'm sorry he involved you in such a tangle. It was not right of him."

"Apparently he told Franklin it wasn't *manly* to have a cairn terrier," Clarissa informed him.

The smile that broke through his seriousness was like the sun appearing. His blue eyes, usually so coolly assessing, sparkled with amusement. "The young gudgeon! No wonder he was sent down. I hadn't the heart to tell him what *I* was sent down for when I was at Oak Knoll. Abducting a dog! And that wasn't even the determining factor, apparently. They jammed the lock on the chapel because they were tired of its being so cold there! The boy has a real future."

"Much like yours," she suggested, her head cocked to one side. "Only I suspect it will be much easier for William to straighten these things out with you than it was for you with your father. You're a deal more approachable than your father was."

Kinsford sighed. "I'm not sure Will thinks so. And I have to admit I haven't always made things comfortable for him. It's funny how I almost find myself behaving like my father, even when I thoroughly disapproved of how he treated me when I was Will's age."

"You have no other example, perhaps."

"That hardly seems an excuse." He brought his gaze back from absentminded contemplation of a bronze candelabra to her face. "You've been a better example, and a better friend, to both my brother and my sister than I have over the years, Miss Driscoll. I find I begrudge that a little."

If this was his way of making amends between them, it was very effective. Clarissa could feel an entirely different sort of tension between them. This had nothing to do with disapproval, but something much more complicated, and personal. She found herself reaching out to lay a hand lightly on his forearm. "You have their love and respect, but they have felt a distance because you're so seldom here. They wish you could spend more time with them."

He covered her hand with his, briefly, withdrawing it when her fingers fluttered uncertainly. "I haven't known how to treat them. I'm not their father, and yet I'm expected to understand what they need. And provide it for them. Fortunately, I'm beginning to remember what it was like to be Will's age.''

He frowned. ''It was actually a confusing time, in many ways. I wanted to be independent and yet I didn't know a damn thing about the world outside school and the estate. I had no money of my own, and my father didn't believe in spoiling his heir by giving me a decent allowance. I couldn't have kept a horse if I hadn't lived at home.''

''Your father was trying to curb your excesses, I imagine. Unfortunately, he overdid it. I know you don't keep William on so short a leash.'' Clarissa smiled encouragingly. ''You seem to have given William the opportunity to manage his own problem this time.''

He was rueful. ''I'm used to taking care of things myself.''

''Sometimes the hardest thing to do is to let someone make his own mistakes and recover from them. But it's often the wisest course.''

''Perhaps that's true of Will. But Aria is another matter entirely. She's only fifteen.''

''And quite a capable girl. She's able to handle the freedom you've given her.''

He shifted uneasily in his chair. ''I probably would have treated Aria differently if I'd known about her mother and . . .'' He let the sentence hang in the air and then, trying to lighten his tone, added, ''I'd probably have acted as though she belonged in a nunnery.''

''Yes, I know.'' Clarissa straightened the white cap on her tidy brown hair. ''You show a decided preference for the women around you behaving like paragons of virtue, Kinsford. Lamentably, not one of us is designed for that role. Not those here in the country, in any case."

Lord Kinsford had the grace to look uncomfortable. "A woman's reputation cannot be restored once destroyed. That's regrettable, but a fact of life, Clarissa."

"I think you overestimate the possibilities for sin in our neighborhood, Kinsford. Really, it's a very quiet village, when all is said and done. I doubt if there are villains waiting to seduce helpless maidens on every country lane. Your sister is relatively safe here."

"I realize that. And I realize that I may have exaggerated the danger of your own situation with regard to your cousin." He corrected himself hurriedly. "Not exaggerated, precisely, but viewed your dancing with him in the least favorable light. I beg your pardon."

"Oh, I don't think you need to beg my pardon, Lord Kinsford. For all you know, I may still turn out to be the village trollop." She gave him an impish impersonation of a scarlet woman, thrusting her hip out and pursing her lips provocatively.

"That's not how they do it at all," he instructed her. "It's done more with the eyes and the feet."

Clarissa looked skeptically at her own feet. "Well, I have shoes on today. I should think it would be far more effective barefoot, as I was the other day when you came."

He laughed. "You did surprise me."

"Possibly the correct word is 'shocked.' You apparently aren't in the habit of being received by ladies without footwear."

"No, but I understand things are done differently in the country," he said, mocking himself. "I shall have to become more familiar with the native habits. Doubtless you will be more than happy to educate me.''

It was a simple comment but somehow its over-tones rang in the room. They regarded each other for long moments. Clarissa could think of no com-ment that would express the odd excitement she felt at his nearness. Kinsford could not begin to sort out his mixed emotions. Above them the dog began to bark and dash about, its nails scratching on the wood floors. With something like relief the earl rose and said, ''I should check on Aria and that unmanage-able dog.''

Unable to speak, Clarissa merely nodded.

Aria was surprisingly spirited and greeted him with, ''Now don't fuss about Max. We were just playing a game.''

''I think he needs a firm hand, Aria, and I doubt you possess one. Perhaps Miss Driscoll could train him a bit before you bring him home.''

Aria pursed her lips and avoided his eyes. ''She likes Max. I can tell. Perhaps I shall bring him with me when I come for my lessons. Once I'm home again, I mean.''

Rather than engage with her in an argument over whether she would continue her lessons, he said, ''Do you think you could come home soon, my dear? You're looking quite fit and I believe Dr. Lawrence is satisfied that the disorientation has passed.''

''Oh, but it hasn't!'' she cried.

His brows rose in surprise. ''Is there some in-stance that you haven't told us about, Aria? That would not do at all, to hide any problems.''

''Well,'' she said, blinking moisture out of her

eyes, "I didn't want to alarm anyone. And it was a small thing. I think it means I am getting better."

"Hmm." Kinsford sat down in the rocking chair and said, "Tell me about it."

"Um, it was this morning. Um, I got out of bed." Aria waved her hands about in a distracted way, looking about the room almost as though she expected the story to be written somewhere on the walls. "I thought I was getting dressed for a carriage ride and I, um, looked in the armoire for my favorite carriage dress. When it wasn't there, I became very concerned and I was about to call for Betty when," she paused dramatically, "suddenly I remembered where I was. So I didn't tell anyone."

"I see," he said, skeptical.

"So I don't think it would be a very good idea for me to go home just yet. Perhaps in another day or so." She cocked her head at him. "You wouldn't mind so very much, would you?"

"We can't impose on Miss Driscoll forever, Aria."

"No, no, of course not. But she doesn't seem to mind, does she? She's really quite the most agreeable person in the world, don't you think?" she asked eagerly.

Kinsford rose from the chair. "She's a remarkable woman," he said, rather obliquely. "Get some rest, Aria."

"Oh, I will," She obediently lay back against the pillows and closed her eyes.

"And behave yourself," Kinsford murmured as he pulled the bedclothes up around her shoulders. Her face in repose looked defenseless and sweetly innocent. He suspected, however, that if she had ever had any disorientation, it certainly hadn't been this morning in searching for a carriage dress. Frowning, he left the room, drawing the door silently closed behind himself.

When Kinsford descended the stairs he found the hallway empty. Meg, who usually appeared instantly at his step, was nowhere to be seen. He could have left then. It would not have been rude, under the circumstances. But he paused only momentarily before striding to the sitting-room door and tapping firmly on the wood panel. Miss Driscoll bid him enter.

She was seated on the sofa doing patching on a sheet. Kinsford was overcome with a sensation of anger—unreasonable, fierce, and consuming anger.

Looking up from her stitching, she regarded him quizzically. "Now what has caused *this* thundercloud? Surely Lady Aria has not put you in such a frame of mind. The poor child is not well and deserves your indulgence."

"It has nothing to do with Aria," he fumed. "Why are you mending a sheet, for God's sake? I can't stand to see you mending a sheet."

"Well, upon my word," she retorted, mincing her syllables like a little old lady. "Am I to throw them away when they are still perfectly usable? Or make dust cloths out of them? Just because you don't wish to see me mending them? My dear Kinsford, you have no idea of the economies to which we are reduced," she teased, with an exaggerated sigh. "Reusing the candle wax, surviving on crusts of bread. We are a sorry lot."

He strode over to the sofa and firmly removed the sheet from her hands. "I'll send you some sheets from the Hall."

"You'll do nothing of the sort," she snapped. "I can manage perfectly well by myself, thank you. I don't mind mending sheets. In fact, it is a very relaxing sort of work. Since Lady Aria has been ill there have been no lessons to keep myself occupied. I have an abhorrence of waste, not a total lack of funds."

"You've just said you are unable to continue your lessons while Aria absorbs your time and remains in the house. I'll reimburse you for any loss of income."

She thrust her needle into the pincushion with unnecessary vigor. "I don't want charity from you, Kinsford."

His eyes blazed. "You know it isn't charity. You're still angry with me for threatening to take the two of them from your care."

"And what if I am?" To her intense mortification, moisture glistened in her eyes. "You have all the power in this situation. You can reduce me to poverty with one careless decision. You can drive me to opening a dame school on a whim. I should hate operating a dame school. But I would do it. I would do it to maintain my household."

He sank onto the sofa beside her and captured her restless hands in his. "For God's sake, Clarissa, I have no intention of ruining you! If taking Aria and Will out of your care would ruin you financially, then you are in far too precarious a position for my liking."

"This has nothing to do with you! Nothing! I have managed all these years and I shall continue to manage." She tried to withdraw her hands from his clasp, but he held firm.

"Listen to me!" He stared into her eyes, willing

her to meet his gaze. "This is another matter I've been remiss in. It was my father who took advantage of yours. He knew Mr. Driscoll's penchant for gaming and played upon it. No, don't argue with me. He knew what he was doing. He wanted to add the Pennhurst land to his estate. There was no excuse for what he did. And I should have realized how desperate your circumstances were when you had to move to this cottage, to teach the local children how to draw and sing. I'll put money in the Funds for you that will give you a decent income, so that you'll be independent at least."

Clarissa shook her head with vigor. "No. If it hadn't been your father, Kinsford, it would have been someone else. I remember thinking, when I was only ten, that I would be lucky if I reached adulthood before we were impoverished." She fought down the ache in her throat. "But my father was such a charming man, so full of life and humor and kindness. Strange, isn't it, that two such different men as our fathers have left us both with difficulties?"

"Not strange at all, probably. They both were excessive in some ways and that is what threatens the next generation." He continued to hold her hands, more lightly now. "But your problem is easily solved, since it is merely financial."

"I can't accept money from you. I'm perfectly capable of earning enough to maintain my household."

Kinsford had no intention of forgetting the matter, but he was willing to let it go for the moment. He considered telling her of his suspicions about his sister, but decided against any revelation at the moment. "Aria is delighted to have Max. She plans to share him with you."

Clarissa smiled and made a deprecatory gesture with her hands. "That's hardly necessary, but very sweet of her."

"Aria has some very endearing traits," Kinsford said.

Clarissa could not bring herself to resume work on mending the sheet after he had left. Her mind was in a turmoil. Despite his reassurances, her existence in the village felt suddenly precarious. And her own emotions were wildly erratic. One moment she felt as drawn to him as she had when he'd kissed her; the next she resolved to put any thought of him out of her mind, as any sensible spinster would do.

Unable to sit still, Clarissa donned a pelisse and set off for Mrs. Luden's shop. They were running low on candles with all the extra activity and guests in her small cottage. And it wouldn't hurt to have a tin of Aria's special biscuits.

Clarissa was startled and mortified when she dug in her purse for the proper coins to have Mrs. Luden say, "No, no. His lordship has taken care of it, Miss Driscoll. He gave me three guineas on account and said you were to have whatever you needed for your household, seeing as Lady Aria was there and making her accustomed demands."

The shopkeeper smiled with delight at the earl's witticism, but Clarissa could feel her cheeks become red with shame. "Nonsense," she returned stoutly. "I am more than able to purchase a few extra candles and biscuits when I have a guest."

Seeing her upset, Mrs. Luden curled Clarissa's fingers back over the coins she was offering and said warmly, "Now don't spoil his generosity, dear. He can well afford it, and I could see it pleased him to have thought of it.''

Clarissa wanted to tell her that she was not interested in pleasing the earl, but it would only have made Mrs. Luden uncomfortable. So she drew a deep breath, controlled her outrage, and smiled blandly at the shopkeeper. ''Well, it was certainly more than thoughtful of Lord Kinsford,'' she said mildly. ''Lady Aria seems to be doing well, but she has certainly made no large demands upon me.''

''I'm ever so glad to hear she's improving. You never know with that kind of fall.'' Mrs. Luden's weathered face creased into a smile. ''She's such a delightful child. And isn't it a rare treat to have all three of them home at once—the earl and both Master William and Lady Aria?''

''It most assuredly is.''

16

Clarissa was furious. Though it was true that Lady Aria's demands on the household budget had been more severe than she had indicated to Mrs. Luden, and that she ordinarily relied on her lessons with the other neighborhood young quality as well to restore her coffers, it was unfathomable to her why Lord Kinsford had concluded that this was an appropriate way in which to relieve her distress. Surely the three guineas could have been sent with William as easily, directly to her, with a pleasant note about their intent to offset the expense of the sister's stay with her. Why would the earl embarrass her by actually leaving money with Mrs. Luden? And had he done it with any other merchant in the vicinity? Clarissa cringed at the thought.

Certainly she had indicated that she wouldn't accept charity from him, but there was a difference between his reimbursing her for legitimate expenses and his setting up a trust fund for her. Couldn't the man see that? What the devil was the matter with him? Clarissa, still in a rage when she returned home, went directly to the sitting room, where she kept paper and quill in the little escritoire she had brought from Pennhurst. In an ecstasy of exquisite fervor she penned:

My dear Lord Kinsford,

Herewith my invoice for five pounds which represents the expense to which I have gone on behalf of your sister. This sum includes the loss of income I have suffered from having Lady Aria in the house, as well as any medicines, extras duties for Meg, etc. I expect payment forthwith, and I expect you to withdraw any monies you may have distributed to local merchants (including Mrs. Luden) with all due haste.

Your most obedient servant,
Clarissa Driscoll

This missive she sent with one of the village lads, hoping the Kinsford Hall butler would supplement the barely adequate coin she was able to give him. Then she spent an hour with Lady Aria, who regarded her rather closely, but asked nothing except, "You seem a trifle agitated, Miss Driscoll. I do hope having me stay here is not disordering your life too badly. Would you rather I went home?"

"Not at all! I'm glad to have you as long as you feel the need to stay here, my dear." Clarissa vigorously pushed back the sleeve of her gown which had caught on the arm of the rocking chair. "I'm sure Lord Kinsford is eager to have you home, however, and you do appear to be much better."

"Oh, yes, but not well enough to leave just yet," Aria declared, alarmed. "Another day or two, I think. Just until I see if I have more episodes of—that problem."

This last was said in a dramatic whisper and Clarissa frowned. Was there something going on here that she was unaware of? She was about to pursue this possibility when Lady Aria sighed and said, "I believe I shall have a little nap now, Miss Driscoll. My head feels a little cottony and a nap will refresh me."

Clarissa rose and tucked her patient in snugly. "Of course. Perhaps you're doing too much in the way of watercolors too soon."

"Oh, but that's what keeps me from being bored," Lady Aria assured her, turning her head on the pillow to make sure that her work-in-progress was not visible. It was, she had assured Clarissa, a surprise. Knowing the girl's penchant for delightful but piercing portrayals, Clarissa felt she could well await the viewing.

When Lord Kinsford presented himself for his evening visit to his sister, Clarissa was not available to him. Meg told him this with a rather nervous air, and Kinsford felt certain the lady of the house was merely hiding in her sitting room. Well, never mind. Her note had been quite explicit on the subject of what she expected and he had brought a purse with the required funds. "Perhaps I will see her before I leave," he said, setting the purse on the hall table.

Meg did not reply and Kinsford raised his brows. "Does she intend to avoid me, then?" he asked.

"I'm sure I wouldn't know, my lord," Meg replied stiffly.

Kinsford shrugged and took the narrow stairs two at a time. He found his sister working at a watercolor, which she pushed under a drawing pad as he entered the room. "What's this?" he teased. "A secret plot?"

Aria flushed and replied, "Not at all. It's just unfinished and I should like to finish it before anyone sees it."

Their visit proceeded quite pleasantly until Kinsford happened to ask Aria if Betty was of some help to her. "For if she's in the way here, she must certainly come home." He added wryly, "Miss Driscoll is quite put out enough with me, without the added burden of an unnecessary servant."

Aria's eyes filled with chagrin. "You *cannot* have put Miss Driscoll out of temper, Kinsford. She is the most accommodating soul on earth! Oh, I knew there was something this afternoon when she sat with me. She was quite distracted. Really, you are the most trying person I know."

Making allowances for her indisposition, Kinsford reined in his own exasperation. "Don't fret about it, Aria. Miss Driscoll and I rub along tolerably well most of the time. I did something meant to be helpful and she misinterpreted my intent. We'll sort it out."

"Well, I certainly hope so," his sister replied, mutinous. "And Will only came to see me once today."

"He went in to Bath for Mr. Alman," Kinsford explained. He had begun to find himself restless and he rose to pace around the small room. "He promised to come first thing tomorrow. Has he told you that he's learning about estate business?"

"Yes, but it's so dreadfully dull," Aria complained. "I wish he would talk of something else."

Kinsford grinned. "You would do well to pay attention, my dear. Will's enthusiasm might be inspiring. You could do worse than to understand a little of it yourself."

"Pooh! Much good it would do me." Aria had some talent at mimickry when she put her mind to it. Now she regaled her brother with an impression of Sir John the magistrate on learning of her newest accomplishment. In his horrified accents she said, "Listen to the girl! Thinks she knows what a drainage ditch is! What next? I suppose pigs will fly."

"I definitely think you're getting better," Kinsford proclaimed. At her obvious apprehension, he added casually, "But it would no doubt be best for you to stay here a little longer. I'll be by in the morning to see you."

Aria's eyes widened. "Are you leaving so soon?"

He had absently picked up a hairbrush from the dressing table, and now laid it back down. "You must be tired. It's late. Your mother sends her love."

"I suppose she's eager for me to be home," Aria said, trying to delay him.

"Yes, very." He bent to kiss her forehead. "I'll give her your love, shall I?"

"Please." As he headed for the door, she said, "Alexander, you *will* sort out your disagreement with Miss Driscoll, won't you?"

"I'll certainly try."

Meg met him at the bottom of the stairs. It seemed to Kinsford that she had been stationed there. "Miss Driscoll is not available," she said, even before he could ask.

"Well, it's important that I see her," he returned in his most imperious voice. "There is a matter about Lady Aria that we must discuss this evening."

Meg looked torn. "Wait here, please," she said

finally, hastening off through the sitting-room door. When she returned, after a low rumble of voices which he could not make out, her cheeks were rosy and her eyes blinked uncertainly. "Miss Driscoll is not available. She said as how you could leave a message with me if there was something urgent. Otherwise, perhaps she would see you in the morning."

"Perhaps!" Kinsford very nearly ground his teeth. Suddenly a thought occurred to him that vexed him so badly he was almost unable to voice his suspicion. "Is there someone with her? Is that notorious cousin here?"

"Oh, no, sir," Meg protested. "We haven't seen Mr. Traling in days, your lordship. Not for days!"

Her denial was adamant and apparently genuine, but Kinsford did not doubt for a moment that Miss Driscoll's servant would lie for her. He had heard no other voice—no male voice—come from the sitting room, but he did not trust that Steven Traling was not there. "I must and I will see Miss Driscoll," he muttered, stomping over to the sitting-room door and throwing it open.

Meg regarded him with open-mouthed astonishment but made no move to stop him. How could she, after all? She was no match for his size and strength. And there was no certainty that he had any harm in mind for her mistress. She did protest, rather sharply, "Oh, no, your lordship, you mustn't. Miss Driscoll will not like it at all. She has most specifically said . . ."

By this time, of course, Kinsford was in possession of a view of the entire sitting-room, with Clarissa seated on the sofa, quite alone, knotting a fringe. Knotting a fringe! Well certainly she was far too busy to see him! Knotting a fringe, indeed!

Clarissa was instantly on her feet. This was adding insult to injury! Her eyes flashed with anger. "If this is the way you intend to behave, Kinsford, you may take your sister from my house this moment. I *will not* have my express instructions disregarded. You have been rude and high-handed and I don't have to tolerate such mannerless behavior."

"Forgive me," he said, though he didn't sound at all penitent. "I didn't mean to alarm you." She looked magnificent. He moved closer to her, capturing a hand unconsciously thrust out to ward him off. "I had to see you."

The color rose further in her cheeks. "You, you, you. I don't care what you needed, Kinsford. This is my house, and I wished not to see you. You had my note. I think I have been perfectly clear about my wishes. Will you please let go of my hand?"

"I find I cannot," he said regretfully. "It seems to belong in mine. Haven't you noticed that?"

Clarissa stared at him. "You have lost your reason, Kinsford. That's the only explanation for this kind of behavior." She tugged unsuccessfully to release her hand. "And I thought it was Lady Aria who was disturbed."

"You are quite the most attractive woman I know," he murmured, lifting her hand to his lips. "I'm sorry about the money. That was foolish of me, but you seemed intent on refusing everything from me."

"I've told you exactly how much you owe me," Clarissa said, watching with bemusement as he continued to press kisses on each of her fingers. "And you've taken care of it in the purse you brought."

"Oh, the money," he said dismissively, turning her now-passive hand over and placing a gentle kiss on the tender palm. "We don't need to talk about the money, Clarissa. We need to talk about us."

"Us." Clarissa felt a tremor run down her spine. "Really, you are being unpardonably foolish." She heard the sitting-room door close, but didn't bother to glance in that direction. Her gaze was entirely captured by the earl's intense expression. "You've forgotten who I am. I'm not that girl by the stile anymore, Alexander. I'm a spinster, without position in county society any longer, without a portion."

"That doesn't matter," he said, capturing her second hand. "I know who you are. I've come to know you over this past week. And yes, you're the girl by the stile, the goddess of spring, and you're a village spinster, and you're a remarkable woman." He ran his lips along her hand, kissing the crook near her thumb. "You're full of life and love and charm and eccentricity. You're the only woman I can imagine spending my life with."

"Spending your life with," she repeated, dazed. His lips were making her feel quite warm and vibrant. There was a catch in her throat when she said, "You've had a distressing week. Next week, next month, when you return to London, it will seem quite different. I will return to being a dowdy, worthy teacher of drawing and pianoforte. You have quite a different life in London."

His entranced eyes glowed warmly. "A very lonely life, Clarissa. Without a woman to argue the merits of the bills I carry before the Lords and partake of her meals with me and share my bed. I had hardly realized what a very dull and unsatisfactory arrangement it was."

"Because it wasn't unsatisfactory," she protested, almost unable to breathe when she heard his words. "You just think that now. The feeling will go away. Time will dim it, as it did before."

"No." The decided nature of his answer spoke volumes. "The feeling never went away. I ignored it. I refused to allow it access to my heart. But it never went away. It was there waiting for me when I saw you again." He drew the shape of her face with his thumb. "Your precious face." His fingers brushed softly across her lips. "Your sweet lips."

"Alexander." Clarissa found she could say no more as his head bent toward hers. His mouth touched hers lightly at first, skimming across her lips, tasting, giving. And then he pressed harder, asking, receiving. She felt her body alight, her lips alive. This was what she had missed, all these years. The sensation of being both whole and shattered, burning and shivering, ecstatic and yet earthly solid.

His arms were around her, his body pressed against hers, his very breath invading her life. She ached for him. "This," he whispered close to her ear, "is passion. This is what you and I can have. This fire is for just the two of us, Clarissa, to burn brightly and consume, and yet be an ember to fan into flame again and again. Because we were always meant to be together."

She shuddered in his arms. And drew back from him, slowly, reluctantly. He allowed her to go, his questioning gaze fastened to her eyes. "What is it, Clarissa?"

"I know you mean well, Alexander. And I know there's some truth to the affection you feel for me." She held her hand up lightly to prevent his speaking. "Just hear me out, please. We've been in close proximity since your sister's injury. That's reminded us of all the 'what might have beens' that we never settled between us.''

He cocked his head quizzingly. "A very fortunate circumstance, I should think."

Clarissa sighed. "Yes, in some ways. But look at the other ways, Kinsford. You are left now with the knowledge that your sister cannot go on as she has been, that your stepmother is not a suitable guide for either your sister or brother, that Will is in need of some direction in his life.'' She leaned back against the wall to give herself a little support. "I am very much afraid that you have unconsciously come to see me as the solution to your problems.''

"What problems?" Kinsford frowned. "You're not suggesting that I'd marry you to provide my sister with a companion, are you? Or my stepmother with a keeper? Or my brother with a teacher?''

Her shoulders rose helplessly. "It's not that you would do it purposely, Alexander. Everything just seems to fall a little too easily into place, doesn't it?'' She ticked the items off on her fingers. "You and I would be married. Then I would come to live at the Hall. Then there would be business that demanded your attention in London. It would be only reasonable that I would stay at the Hall to chaperone your sister. Certainly your stepmother could not be left alone there, even if you were to take Will or Aria to town. It makes so much *sense*.''

"How I feel about you doesn't make the least sense," he protested, bending to kiss the tip of her nose. "Except that it is so very natural and right. These are all unnecessary doubts, my dear. They have nothing to do with the way I feel about you.''

Ignoring his words, if not his kiss, Clarissa continued, "Then there is the matter of your feeling guilt about your father taking advantage of mine, and your wanting to provide me with financial security because of that. And the children's affection for me. They would be pleased by your marrying me, I suppose."

"You suppose! I think Aria has planned this from the day I arrived home," he interjected, grinning provocatively. "Clarissa, Clarissa, all these things are unimportant. All of them have other solutions. Surely you can see that."

"Yes, but marrying me is the *best* solution." She ducked her head when he attempted to kiss her again. "Alexander, you've let yourself succumb to a romantic fantasy that might have worked ten years ago. Not now. I've been alone for a long time. I have my own cottage, modest as it is. I'm used to having my own way. I don't have to prostrate myself to the whims of propriety. I lead my own life. Can you understand that? Or does it seem to you that leading my own life cannot possibly compete with being married to an earl and fashioning my life around him and around his interests and his family and his estate?"

Kinsford refused to be provoked. "It seems to me that you should wish to be held by one particular earl, and kissed by him, and even irritate him beyond bearing on occasion. It seems to me that you should marry me and love me for the rest of your life."

His arms were on either side of her now, hands on the wall, framing her like a portrait. Clarissa felt a twinge of anticipation race through her body as he lowered his lips to hers. For long moments her mind was clouded with a haze of euphoria that would not release her to consider his proposal clearly. Reluctantly, she squirmed out from under his arms and stood with her back to him.

"I'll have to think about all this, Kinsford," she murmured. "I'll need some time to figure out what's really happening here."

His eyes danced. "Don't you know? Well, I suppose I must not tease you further tonight. From start to finish I have behaved most unscrupulously this evening and you deserve a chance to consult your own feelings." He moved behind her but merely bent to kiss the top of her head. "I trust you will find them quite as strong as my own, my dear. Until tomorrow."

It was no use trying to think about what had happened, Clarissa found as she moved from sofa to chair to escritoire to window in the sitting room. Meg had appeared once to inquire, with a most suspicious light lurking in her eyes, whether she could be of any further assistance to Miss Driscoll that evening. Clarissa had sent her off to bed. And in due time, she herself climbed the stairs to her room.

But she could not seem to rid her mind of the wild variety of sensations she had been assailed with that evening. Much as she wished to review the events with rational clarity, she was unable to do so. Clarissa had never felt this way before, either physically or emotionally. She had never been held in a man's arms and experienced the response of her body to his touch. She had been offered a chance at love, security, and position all in one breath, as it were.

Why? Did Kinsford really love her, or delude himself because it would be convenient to marry her? Clarissa drew the brush through her hair again and again, unable to reach any conclusion because every time she was distracted by her body's memory of delight.

17

Steven Traling had been particularly unhappy that morning with the way his in-laws were treating him. They barely allowed him to see his poor wife, who was due to produce a child at any moment. "You mustn't excite her," Mrs. Wilton had insisted. As though he would do anything to disturb Jane's well-being! Surely his wife would want him to be there to sustain her during this period before her ordeal. But she was not strength enough against her mother's insistence that there was no place for Mr. Traling in the proceedings, or even during the wait.

Miffed, Steven had departed.

He had ridden to the outskirts of Pennwick before he remembered that Miss Driscoll still had Lady Aria staying with her. But he was in no mood to have one more female dictate what he could or could not do that day. So he continued on to the cottage, pleased to see on arriving that at least there were no other horses outside the small house. In his opinion, humble as it was, Lord Kinsford was there entirely too often for Miss Driscoll's peace of mind.

Something had been happening to Clarissa over this last week. Steven recognized that she was not quite as available to him as she had once been, and he suspected that it was not entirely due to the demands of Lady Aria. He guessed that the earl's threat to cease the children's instruction with her, which would make it very difficult for Clarissa to survive, was distressing her more than she let on.

Steven was shown into the sitting room where Clarissa greeted him with mild disquiet. "What are you doing here, Steven?" she asked, her brows raised slightly. "Isn't it almost time for Jane to have the baby?

"Yes, but no one wants me around," he grumbled. "So they can very well do without me."

"I hope you've left your direction with someone."

"You sound like a schoolmistress, Clarissa." He sat down and drew his gloves through restless fingers. "Yes, I've left my direction, more or less. In an emergency I could be found."

Clarissa merely waited for him to continue. She was decidedly distracted and not entirely paying attention to him. "What am I to do with them?" he demanded eventually. "I can't go on forever not being master in my own home. Surely you can see that."

Clarissa absently shifted a watercolor pad on the table beside her. "Perhaps men make too much of being masters in their own homes."

"What! A man's home is his castle," Steven cried, only half in jest. "Look at you. I don't think you even realize how important it is to you to have this cottage. And not even a real companion to challenge your authority. Very few women have that kind of independence."

Startled, Clarissa looked at him sharply, but could see no evidence of hidden significance to his words. With a sigh, she said, "Yes, it is very important to me. I should very much dislike having to give it up.''

"He's not threatening you again, is he?" Steven demanded, his hands unconsciously forming fists. "He wouldn't dare withdraw your livelihood after all you've done for his sister during her illness."

"No, he's not threatening me."

Steven relaxed and smiled at her. "Well, he'll be off to London in no time and things will return to normal."

Clarissa fingered the pages of the watercolor pad without looking at him. "The children need his guidance, Steven, even if he's not their father. Their mother is hopeless and I don't have any real authority with them other that what they grant me. He would have to make some arrangement for their care."

The door to the sitting room flew open and there stood Lady Aria in an astonishing outfit. She had draped a coverlet about her person in a most artistic manner. Then, finding that she rather liked the effect, had piled her hair upon her head and tossed a few pieces from Clarissa's modest jewelry collection into her locks. She stood there triumphantly, smiling benignly on the two of them.

"I've decided to go to the ball after all," she explained regally. "I know you wished me to, and I fear I was being a bit stubborn because I didn't really want to encounter Sir James there. He's such a dreadful bore and he will prose on and on at me, to say nothing of asking me to stand up with him more than twice! I'm so glad Will has agreed to chaperone me. He'll be able to keep all the stupid young pups away from me for long enough to let me breathe, don't you think?''

Steven turned astonished eyes to Clarissa, who remained seated as she regarded the girl. "My dear Lady Aria, you look delightful but I'm afraid William hasn't arrived yet."

"Hasn't arrived yet?" Lady Aria frowned, her hand going up to secure a pendant that had been twisted around a forelock of hair. "But he was supposed to take me. What am I to do?"

By this time Clarissa had determined that Lady Aria was *not* having a spell of disorientation. The outfit was too ludicrous, the eyes too full of mischief to deceive her. But with Steven there, Clarissa was not about to call the little minx on her subterfuge.

"Perhaps it would be best if you waited in your room for him, my dear. I dare say he won't be long." Clarissa moved to take her patient's elbow and Lady Aria reluctantly allowed herself to be propelled out into the hall.

As they began to cross to the stairs, there was a hurried rapping on the front door. Clarissa was not anxious to have any visitors at the moment. Meg arrived in the hallway, took one glance at Lady Aria and paled. Steven stood in the doorway of the sitting room, looking helpless. The knock came louder on the front door.

"Steven! Are you in there, Steven?" demanded a soft but insistent female voice.

"Oh, my God, it's Jane," he said.

Meg looked to Clarissa for guidance. "Well, you will certainly have to let her in," Clarissa sighed, shrugging helplessly at Steven. "Surely she cannot have come here in her state! You must be mistaken."

But he was most assuredly correct, as he should be in recognizing his own wife's voice. As Meg quickly drew open the door, a very small and very enceinte young woman was revealed, her eyes blinking back tears of distress.

"But look," Lady Aria exclaimed. "She's about to have a baby. How did she get here? Is she one of Kinsford's lovers, do you suppose?"

"No, I do not suppose," Clarissa said, sternly hushing the young woman. "This is Mr. Traling's wife, Jane."

Steven had dashed forward and pulled his wife across the threshold of the cottage. Outside he could see his in-laws' carriage, but he caught no glimpse of anyone else in the vehicle. "You haven't brought your mother?" he asked, both alarmed and relieved. "What are you doing here, Jane?"

"You shouldn't have left me at a time like this," she protested as she allowed herself to be lowered into a chair Meg thrust forward for her use. The maid uttered something about going into the kitchen to get the young lady a glass of tea or water, and disappeared with one brief, scandalized look at her mistress.

Steven was kneeling beside his wife, clasping her hands in his, trying to get the words out that he meant to say. "But I did want to stay with you. Your mother refused to let me. I would have stayed, I swear I would have stayed. You didn't tell your mother that you wanted me to stay."

"But I *did*. I most certainly did. Didn't she tell you?" Jane was quite adamant in her protestations, and everyone hung on the gentle insistence of her words, so they were quite aware when a look of pain overcame her face and she bent forward and clasped her abdomen.

"Do you suppose that the carriage ride has brought on my time, Steven?" she asked almost meekly.

"Several times on the way here I had these feelings of pain that could be the child coming, you see. Perhaps I should not have come."

"No, of course you shouldn't have come," he said, but not in a scolding way, more out of fear and worry for her safety. "I don't think we can take you back in this condition, Jane. Not if the child is coming. You'll have to stay."

"Well," said Lady Aria, excited by the possibilities here, "you shall have my room for your wife, Mr. Traling. It's a delightful room, if not particularly large. And we shall send for the midwife. Don't you think so, Miss Driscoll?"

Clarissa, amused at this abrupt return to practicality, agreed. "But Mrs. Traling shall have my bedchamber. Meg can prepare it for her straightaway."

"I don't believe I shall go to the ball after all," Lady Aria declared. "You do have the most fascinating household, Miss Driscoll."

"It never used to be," Clarissa said dampeningly.

There was a knock at the door. Clarissa had a moment of supreme desire to be elsewhere, then descended to answer the summons herself, since Meg had not returned from the nether regions, and Steven had disappeared. On the doorstep stood William, resplendent in a hussar's uniform.

"I knew you would look quite dashing in uniform," Lady Aria cried.

When William saw his sister, he exclaimed, "What the devil are you wearing, Aria? You look ludicrous."

Before his sister could answer, there was a moan of pain from the lady seated to his left in the hallway. The young man turned to her, blinked his eyes uncertainly and said, "Can I help you, ma'am?"

At that moment Mr. Traling issued forth from the kitchen with Meg, her sister Betty, and a cup of tea which he insisted on carrying himself. "Here, my dear," he said, as though it were exactly what she was waiting for. "This will be just the ticket."

Betty removed the cup from his hands and told him that they had much better see my lady up to a bed than to be feeding her cups of tea at this moment. Steven looked as if he meant to take exception to this advice, but sighed and swooped his wife into his arms. "Just show us the way, Clarissa."

His hostess, after tossing a brief glance skyward, did indeed lead the party up the stairs and into her own room. The sunlight poured through partially open windows, making the room bright and fresh smelling.

"What a lovely room!" Jane Traling exclaimed. "I wish my room were so bright and airy. There is nothing so stuffy as the way my mother has kept the house all these years. And even though the fashion has changed, she will not come round to seeing that it is healthier for one to have fresh air than stifling air in a room."

Steven, who wondered if this criticism of her mother was something that only the pains of childbirth had induced, helped settle Jane on the bed. "We should have a small house of our own," he suggested, taking advantage. "Just a small place, but one where we could have sunlight for ourselves, and for the children."

"Now that will be enough talking, ma'am," Betty cautioned. "You'll need your strength for the work you have to do here. The gentleman will not want to be staying here with you until all is over and done with."

"But I do," Steven protested. "At least until I would be in the way. That's what I've always wanted to do." And he held tightly to his wife's hand.

Clarissa prevented William from following her into the room. "No, my dear, this is no place for you." She closed the door and directed him into Aria's room. "Just be sure the dog is under control, will you?"

"Aria seems quite capable of that," William remarked, watching as his sister placed the animal on a pillow she had covered with a cloth from the dressing table. "You may be wondering why . . ."

They heard a loud hammering at the front door. Clarissa was not about to entertain any more guests. The upstairs of her cottage at least, was bursting at the seems. When she glanced out the window of Aria's room, however, she could see that it was Lady Kinsford at the door. Reluctantly she left brother and sister to fend for themselves and went to admit her ladyship.

"You cannot keep her from me," Lady Kinsford insisted as she elbowed her way into the hall. "I am the child's mother and I *will* see her, this instant."

Clarissa, torn between amusement and despair, dipped her head and agreed. "If you will come this way, Lady Kinsford. Lady Aria is upstairs in her room."

"Her room! Her room is at the Hall, not in this shabby little cottage," Lady Kinsford informed Clarissa as Meg helped relieve the woman of her pelisse and walking stick. Not that Lady Kinsford had walked. There was now a second carriage outside the cottage, in addition to Steven Traling's horse. Clarissa thought it looked as though she were running a stable.

"Come with me, please," she offered and led the way up the precipitous stairs, hoping that Lady Kinsford would not trip on her long robes and tumble down the short flight.

At the head of the stairs they were met by a wail from Clarissa's bedroom as Jane Traling suffered a pang of labor. Lady Kinsford clutched her breast and cried, "What are you doing to the poor child?"

"That's another guest of mine, who is in childbed," Clarissa informed her in an offhand manner meant to disarm the woman.

"In childbed? Here? Do you run a boardinghouse?" Lady Kinsford demanded. "I don't believe I knew you ran a boardinghouse. What is my daughter doing in such a place?"

"Oh, Mama," Lady Aria called from her room, where she was feeding Max tidbits from the breakfast tray. "Come and see my new dog. His name is Max."

"My poor child! What have they done to you?" Lady Kinsford's eyes had widened considerably at the sight of Aria in her outlandish outfit. "They have taken away your clothes! They are treating you as a lunatic!"

"Hush, Mama," Lady Aria insisted. She dusted her hands together to rid them of crumbs and said stoutly, "I've just been dressing up. Will can tell you."

"Will? Is Will here, too?"

William, who had been hiding behind the door, now stepped forward to confront his mother. "Yes, indeed I am here, ma'am. I have been keeping a constant watch over my sister and no harm has befallen her here."

"How can you say that? She is at that this moment

in a boardinghouse where strange women give birth to children, probably out of wedlock. This is not the place for any daughter of mine to be found." Lady Kinsford glared at Clarissa, who merely returned her look with a slight twitching at the corners of her lips. "Aria must be removed at once!"

"I think we must consult Kinsford about that, ma'am." Will suggested. "He has instructed that she stay here."

"And does Kinsford know that a woman is giving birth next door to your sister?" his mother demanded, her eyes taking on a cunning look. "Perhaps this has something to do with him. I am not at all happy that he hasn't as yet married. It's not a good thing for a young man to be at loose ends at his age. How could it be? His father was married far younger. And married soon after Kinsford's mother died as well. It's not wise for these country gentlemen to be left to their own devices."

William looked despairingly at Clarissa, who said, "The lady giving birth next door is my cousin's wife, Lady Kinsford. It's indeed unfortunate that this should have happened with Lady Aria here, but it cannot be helped. Please let me take you down to the sitting room and Meg will get you a cup of tea."

There was another wail from the next room and Lady Kinsford grasped the doorknob where her hand rested. "I don't understand how you can allow such a thing to happen. People just do not come to one's house to give birth."

William took his mother's elbow and turned her toward the stairs. "Now, Mama. You mustn't let yourself be distressed. Miss Driscoll is more than capable of taking care of everything."

"But she's never had a child herself. She cannot

possibly be capable of taking care of everything. You have no idea, William. Childbirth is a nasty, painful business and an unmarried woman should be nowhere in the vicinity. I assure you it is best that the young have no idea of what is involved or they would never in their lives become married and have children.''

18

Clarissa helped William guide his mother down the stairs, where they found Meg just ascending with warmed cloths and hot water. Clarissa left William with his mother while she went to prepare a cup of tea for the dowager. When she returned, her guest had not finished elaborating on the miseries of childbirth.

"I tell you it is most unreasonable to expect a poor, helpless female to go through that kind of pain," she was telling William, who looked thoroughly discomfited. "Not that I begrudge you and your sister the difficulties, mind, but it does seem to me that things could have been arranged a little differently. After all, one is imposed upon quite enough by the act of procreating."

It seemed to occur to her that this was not perhaps something she should be discussing with her son, but William's eyes danced as he leapt up to help Miss Driscoll with the tea things. Soon enough Lady Kinsford forgot that he was there, though, in her meditations.

"Perhaps my mother was remiss in not telling me certain things that she should have," she opined. "If I had known what to expect! But I really did not and it was the most horrifying thing, you see. Not that your father was not the most perfect gentleman. Certainly he was. And thoughtful of me in every way. But to have expected me to bear two children when he already had an heir! Still, it is the way of the world. Or at least of men,'' she lamented. ''One has to do one's duty.''

''Indeed, ma'am,'' William murmured. ''Should you like sugar in your tea?''

Lady Kinsford looked up at him as though puzzled to find him there. ''Yes, I always take two sugars. You know, William, this is not the time of year you should be home from school, is it? I had thought it wouldn't be time for a break from Oak Knoll for some weeks.''

''A small matter of being sent down,'' William explained without the least embarrassment. ''Nothing that can't be rectified, I assure you. Kinsford has already spoken to me on the subject. In fact, there are several matters which he is at present attending to.''

''Well, he is not the man his father was,'' she said with a sigh. ''Always away in London and sending notes to his bailiff. That was not the way his father ran the estate. I should very much like to see him take more of an interest.''

''And I think he will,'' William replied, casting a surprisingly sharp glance at Miss Driscoll. ''He seems to have found an interest in the country recently. And there is Aria to be considered.''

''The poor child. I'll send over more clothes for her. What can she be thinking of, wrapping herself up in such shoddy draperies? Is she all right?''

Though Lady Kinsford looked to her son for an answer, it was Clarissa who responded. ''We think she is progressing fairly well. In fact, I feel certain

Dr. Lawrence will recommend her return to the Hall very shortly.''

"It's been much quieter here for her than at the Hall," William explained.

At that moment there was a long, drawn-out cry of pain from the room above them. They heard a door close above and a man's footsteps proceed heavily down the stairs. Steven Traling appeared surprised to see so many people when he entered the sitting room. "They won't let me stay any longer," he complained.

"They'll take good care of her," Clarissa assured him. And seeing her means of escape, she added, "It might be an excellent idea if I were to go up and offer my assistance." Fortunately, for all the help she could be, the midwife arrived as she hurried through the hall. Relieved, Clarissa bore her upstairs to the needy Jane.

When Lady Kinsford requested seedcake, Mr. Traling instantly offered to find it. Meg and Betty were both upstairs, with Miss Driscoll and the midwife. Mr. Traling was happy to be of any service that would take him out of the dowager's immediate vicinity. He hunted through the various cabinets in the kitchen until he came to the metal box that contained the seedcake. As he sliced off several large pieces, he happened to look out the back window and saw Lord Kinsford riding toward Miss Driscoll's cottage. Mr. Traling let himself out the back door and waved the earl to the back of the building.

"You could tie the horse here," he suggested. "It's rather crowded out front."

Kinsford swung down from Longbridge. "You here again?" he asked with slight acerbity.

"Yes, this is not a day when poor Clarissa is going to get any peace."

The previous day Kinsford might have allowed the familiarity to distress him. Now he merely asked, "Why not?"

"There are quite a few people here requiring her attention. My wife Jane, for instance, is in the midst of giving birth. Which of course required a midwife who arrived some while ago. Jane is in Clarissa's bedchamber, and Lady Aria is in Miss Snolgrass's room catering to the dog Max. Her mama is in the sitting room waiting for seedcake and reminiscing about the birth of her children. William, in a hussar's uniform, is there with her."

"A regular May Day festival," Kinsford murmured. "Poor Miss Driscoll."

At which moment there was a different sort of cry from the room upstairs, that of a newborn babe.

When Mr. Traling had disappeared upstairs, Kinsford presented himself in the sitting room with the seedcake the younger man had cut. His stepmama regarded him with confusion.

"I didn't know you were here, Kinsford," she said, frowning. "What happened to that other fellow?"

"Mr. Traling has gone up to see his new child." He raised his brows at William, lounging in the old hussar's uniform.

Aria told me to wear it," William protested. "Remember, it was in the trunk in the north attic. Perhaps she was having one of her disoriented phases," he suggested, not meeting Kinsford's eyes.

"Hmmm." He turned back to his stepmother. "Is there anything I can get you, ma'am?"

His stepmother sighed. "Women die in childbirth, you know. Lots of women. You live in fear that you will die, or the child, or that you will have to have another one and bear all that pain. I became pregnant once when Will was ten, you know. The thought of having another child terrified me. I had nightmares about its tearing me apart."

She set down her teacup and wrung her hands in her lap. "And then I miscarried. The earl was very disappointed, and I felt wretchedly guilty, as though my fear had brought it on. I don't think that could be true, do you?"

William, to whom this discourse seemed to have been directed, dropped down beside his mother on the sofa and clasped her hand tightly in his own. "No, I'm quite certain that it could not have done that, Mama. These things happen in the course of nature."

Lady Kinsford nodded, her head slightly cocked to one side. "Your father was angry, you see. He thought I had not taken good care of myself. Though why he so particularly wanted another child, I cannot imagine."

"Perhaps he thought that none of the ones he had already gotten were quite what he expected," William suggested, glancing at Kinsford with obvious affinity.

"Perhaps." Lady Kinsford also shifted her attention to Kinsford. "Things were never the same after that," she mused, fingering the folds of her own gown with agitated fingers. "Nothing seemed quite to please him any more . . . and no one. It was very distressing. Very distressing."

"Of course it was," Kinsford agreed, feeling a slight understanding of his stepmother for the first time in years. "Let me get Aria, and then I will send the three of you home. We mustn't clutter up Miss Driscoll's house any longer."

Lady Kinsford's face softened into a smile. "Can we take Aria home, then? How nice. She should change, though. She looks a fright."

William grinned at Kinsford's questioning look. "You'll see."

The earl found his sister in a most extraordinary costume indeed, with the dog beside her and a watercolor pad on her lap. "Oh, Kinsford, we have been having the most famous time," Aria cried at sight of him. "Mrs. Traling has had a baby boy and Miss Driscoll is going to bring him in for me to see in a minute."

"I see." He folded himself into the rocking chair, as he had on so many previous occasions. "Was this costume intended to convince me of another episode of disorientation, Aria?"

Aria giggled, not at all discomposed by his knowledge of the truth. "Lord, it seems ages ago. When I heard someone come, I thought it was Will and I went dashing downstairs. I had sent him a note asking him to wear the hussar's uniform. He looks quite dashing, doesn't he? I had decided I would say we were going to a ball because then I could get dressed up. You know, I don't think Miss Driscoll quite believed me, either."

"I'm not surprised," Kinsford said dryly. "She's not easily hoodwinked."

Aria regarded him curiously, then shoved the watercolor toward him. "This is what I've been working on for the last few days. What do you think?"

All the characters in the drama were there: Kinsford,

and William, and Max, and Steven Traling (Aria was working on his wife), and Miss Driscoll, and the maids Meg and Betty, and Lady Kinsford, and Dr. Lawrence. The drawing was a doll's house view of the cottage, with the characters in various rooms, but Lady Aria herself in each room with whoever was there. It was a charming collage of scenes. "Of course, I shall have to add the baby once I've seen him," she said.

"What a charming collage!" Kinsford exclaimed. "I suppose this is me, standing over Miss Driscoll wagging my finger."

Aria ducked her head impishly. "You simply would not believe what a superb creature she is."

"It has merely taken me a little longer to learn, Aria. I haven't, after all, spent as much time as you have in the country."

"More's the pity," murmured his sister.

Kinsford ruefully agreed. "I have a mind to spend more time here."

"I had hoped you would." Aria took back the watercolor pad and ran a finger over the scene of her with bandaged head in the sitting room after the accident. "You're not angry with me about my little deception, are you, Alexander?"

Before he could answer, Clarissa appeared at the door, holding a small infant wrapped in a soft blanket. The child's tiny fingers were just visible, and its face was red from crying and the exhaustion of being born. Mr. Traling was right behind her.

"Why, he's beautiful," Aria exclaimed, earning her Steven's undying gratitude, for the child looked quite ugly to him. Not at all the soft-edged little angel he had expected.

Steven, without taking his eyes from his son, said,

"I'm dreadfully sorry we've taken up your bedchamber, Clarissa. And I don't suppose Jane can be moved for a while."

"I'll find a spot in the sitting room," Clarissa replied. "Sometimes one's house does not seem *quite* large enough."

Kinsford found that Clarissa was avoiding his eyes, but he only smiled. "There's no need for that, Miss Driscoll. As soon as Aria changes into proper clothes, she and Will are taking their mother back to the Hall."

"Are we?" Aria asked, disappointed. "But I should like very much to stay and play with the baby, Kinsford."

"Perhaps another day," he replied. "The baby is a little young for so much excitement. I'm sure Mr. Traling wishes to return him to his mother. And while you're changing, Aria, Miss Driscoll and I are going to take Max for a walk."

"Are we?" Clarissa asked uncertainly.

"We are." Kinsford decreed.

Clarissa might have protested, but she did not really object to accompanying his lordship from the cottage. She threw a blue shawl about her shoulders and allowed Kinsford to tie the lead about the dog's neck.

When the front door closed behind them, Kinsford tucked Clarissa's hand under his arm and began to walk down the lane toward the fields. The day was a little cooler than it had been earlier, and there was a wispy breeze, but the sun shone brightly. Clarissa peeked up at Kinsford, to see what she could read of his face, and found that he was gazing down at her with a most intriguing light in his eyes.

Her heart *would* dance in her breast, and she swallowed hard against a sudden and unexpected swell of tears. It had been such a very long time since she had fallen in love with Alexander Barrington. It had been for such a very long time that she had denied that love, or even the remotest interest in this self-contained, slightly haughty, strong, and wonderful man.

In an expectant but companionable silence they walked toward Clarissa's old home of Pennhurst. Just as it came in sight, they reached the stile where Kinsford had kissed her so many years ago. "Here," he said, and motioned to the grassy hillock on their right. They seated themselves there, with Max snuffling busily about the bushes, tugging again and again at the lead. Eventually Kinsford, with a shrug of his shoulders, let the lead go and allowed the dog to wander off on his own. "If he gets lost it will serve him right. I dare say you never wanted him in your house at all."

"I've grown accustomed to him," Clarissa admitted. "But it's Aria who has fallen in love with him. She would be devastated if he didn't come back."

"Oh, he'll come back. Never fear. The animal has a very good sense of what is good for him. He even cozied up to me when Franklin brought him to the Hall."

"No!" Clarissa grinned at him. "Surely the animal didn't realize your importance or he would never have been so presumptuous."

"Are you mocking me?" He lifted her hand to his lips. "I find that I like that, from you. Have I told you how dearly I love you?"

"But, Alexander . . ."

"Well, if I haven't, I shall tell you now. I am head

over ears in love with you. I shan't be able to sleep, or eat, or ride if you don't agree to marry me.'' He kissed the tip of her nose. "I know you fear you will lose your independence. But, my dearest, just look at my stepmama. She does precisely what she wishes, says anything that comes to her mind. Being Lady Kinsford does not necessarily inhibit one's creativity, does it?''

Clarissa shook her head with amusement. "I must admit I had never looked at it in quite that light. It's not that I don't love you, Alexander,'' she admitted softly. "I do love you. When I see you, I am sometimes quite overcome with emotion. And I think of you when you're not with me. But . . .''

"But it would make a change in your life, and you are not certain it is entirely advantageous.'' He studied her with those intense eyes. "I dare say it won't all be advantageous, Clarissa. There will be onerous duties as a countess, and some constriction of your freedom. Still, you would have my very great encouragement to lead the kind of life you wished.''

"You might forget that if I did something outrageous. Or you might be called back to London and leave me to sort things out here,'' she argued, but weakly. He was running a finger tenderly over the contours of her face.

"If I forget, you will remind me. If I leave for London, I will leave with you. I promise, Clarissa.'' He pulled her tightly against his strong chest. "We'll make things work together, because I know I am asking a lot—for you to take on a husband and two rambunctious young people, and an odd and irascible stepmother-in-law. To say nothing of a dog of questionable discrimination.''

Max had charged up to them and now barked sharply, but they ignored him. Clarissa pulled back from the earl's hold a little to protest, "But you were very irritated with me when you first came to see me last week. Don't you see that that could happen again?"

"You were doing everything for the children that I should have been doing. I couldn't bear to think of it, especially after what my family had done to you." When she started to speak, he released her and touched a finger to her lips. "Just remember this one thing. If you don't wish to marry me, there will still be an annuity for you. I could do no less after what you've done for us. You don't have to take on this short-tempered, unreasonable man if you really don't love him."

Her eyes shone with amusement and a deep affection. "Oh, Kinsford, I don't know how I would manage anymore without you around. I cannot bear the thought of your returning to London again, leaving me alone here. Just the way I've always been, and yet not at all as I was. Everything has changed."

He drew her to him again, holding her for a long moment before releasing her. "I had no idea I could feel this way about anyone. And I'm afraid I'm not always much good at it; I've been jealous and contrary instead of generous and agreeble. Will you bear with me?"

"Yes," she said, her eyes full of the warmth and openness that he loved and needed. "You're certainly the most challenging person I've ever loved, but I love you in such a very special way that I dare say we shall rub along quite well, my dear."

When he bent to kiss her, Max ran round and

round where they were seated, barking excitedly. But it was several minutes before they paid him the least heed, and then only to scoop him up between them and tell him to hush.